Praise for the Lila Maclean

THE SEMESTER OF OU

"The best cozy debut I've read this year. An engaging heroine, a college setting that will have you aching to go back to school, and a puzzler of a mystery make this a must-read for cozy lovers."

– Laura DiSilverio,
National Bestselling Author of the Readaholics Book Club Series

"A pitch-perfect portrayal of academic life with a beguiling cast of anxious newbies, tweedy old troublemakers and scholars as sharp as they're wise. Lila's Stonedale is a world I'm thrilled to have found. Roll on book two!"

– Catriona McPherson,
Multi-Award-Winning Author of the Dandy Gilver Series

"A very intricate, cool story featuring the depth of an institution where everyone is dying to climb the ladder of success."

– *Suspense Magazine*

"Takes the reader into higher education's secrets and shadows, where the real lesson is for the new professor—how to stay alive. If you're smart, you'll read this book."

– Lori Rader-Day,
Anthony Award-Winning Author of *The Black Hour*

"College professor Lila Maclean gets an A+ for her detecting skills in this twisty mystery set at a Colorado university. With suspects and motives galore, solving the murder of department chair Roland Higgins won't be easy, but Lila's got brains and guts to spare. A great book."

– Maggie Barbieri,
Author of the Murder 101 Series

THE ART OF
VANISHING

The Lila Maclean Academic Mystery Series
by Cynthia Kuhn

THE SEMESTER OF OUR DISCONTENT (#1)
THE ART OF VANISHING (#2)

THE ART OF VANISHING

A Lila Maclean Academic Mystery

Cynthia Kuhn

HENERY PRESS

THE ART OF VANISHING
A Lila Maclean Academic Mystery
Part of the Henery Press Mystery Collection

First Edition
Trade paperback edition | February 2017

Henery Press, LLC
www.henerypress.com

Trade Paperback ISBN-13: 978-1-63511-169-9
Digital epub ISBN-13: 978-1-63511-170-5
Kindle ISBN-13: 978-1-63511-171-2
Hardcover Paperback ISBN-13: 978-1-63511-172-9

Printed in the United States of America

For my family

ACKNOWLEDGMENTS

Thank you to the following...

Kendel Lynn, Art Molinares, Erin George, Rachel Jackson, and everyone at Henery Press—for fantastic, thoughtful guidance. You are all superstars and lovely people! Special shout-out to Erin George, who edits like a dream and always responds to my overly plentiful queries both efficiently and compassionately.

The Hen House—for all of your collegiality and support. Chicken hugs!

Readers and bloggers who have welcomed Lila and/or have introduced her around. Very grateful for you.

Sisters in Crime, Mystery Writers of America, International Thriller Writers, Colorado Authors' League, Women Who Write the Rockies, and Mysteristas. Appreciate the inspiration and community.

Friends and colleagues responsible for assorted kindnesses during the writing of this book (adore you all): Jill Adams, Dru Ann, Gretchen Archer, James Aubrey, Maggie Barbieri, Donnell Bell, Francelia Belton-Briscoe, Mary Birk, Peg Brantley, Becky Clark, Theresa Crater, Laura DiSilverio, Karen Docter, Sandra Maresh Doe, Sebastian Doherty, Margarita Barceló Flores, Erin Webster Garrett, Elsie Haley, LS Hawker, Nancy Hightower, Lorna

Hutchison, Sybil Johnson, Maria Kelson, Mylee Khristoforov, Ryan Lambert, Kate Lansing, Mindy Richards Louviere, Russell McDermott, Catriona McPherson, Jason Miller, Josie and Stuart Mills, Barbara Nickless, Mikkilynn Olmstead, Jon Pinnow, Keenan Powell, Jordyn Redwood, Christy and Bob Rowe, Craig Svonkin, Art Taylor, Wendy Tyson, LynDee Walker, and Kristopher Zgorski. And extra thanks to my incredibly generous readers: Ellen Byron, Marla Cooper, Wendy Crichton, Dotty Guerrera, Jennifer Kincheloe, Ann Myers, Shawn Peterka, Renée Ruderman, Hank Phillippi Ryan, and Diane Vallere.

My beloved family: Guerreras, Kuhns, Crichtons, West-Repperts, Peterkas, Hundertmarks, Abneys, and Welshs. Hugs, gratitude, and much love. (To my amazing mom, dad, sister, and husband, who have been reading and cheering me on forever, no words can adequately express my heartfelt thanks. Also: apologies for subjecting you to so many unsolicited poems over the decades.)

And to Kenneth, Griffin, and Sawyer: a million thanks for your endless patience and encouragement. And for being your wonderful selves (and my sunshine)...love you so much.

Chapter 1

The campus was cloaked in pale gray light. Softly descending flakes muted the frozen landscape and cast a tranquil spell, as if I were inside of a snow globe.

Until a booming voice shattered that all to bits.

"Dr. Maclean, I presume?" Trawley Wellington, former literature professor and current Stonedale University chancellor, descended the stairs of Randsworth Hall, where the muckety mucks were housed—him being the muckiest of them all. "Might I have a word?"

I paused. Chancellor-speak tended to be gentled versions of direct actions, like "have a word" instead of "insist that you report for reprimand" or "borrow you for a minute" rather than "command you to scurry to my side." Although they sounded polite, they were iron-clad demands, make no mistake.

"Hello, Chancellor," I said, waiting until he had reached the bottom step. He didn't move to the sidewalk but remained literally and metaphorically above me. As he intended. I don't know why he thought he needed the step—at well over six feet tall, he already looked down on most of us anyway, and his uncanny resemblance to Franklin Delano Roosevelt augmented his air of authority. "I was on my way to Crandall Hall to deliver the materials," he informed me.

At my blank look, he made a sound of exasperation. "You're on the Arts Week committee, are you not, Lila?"

"Yes," I said. "Arts Week" was an abbreviated version of the official title, "Twenty-First Century Arts and Culture Series," during which notable individuals taught workshops and gave creative readings or lectures. It was very popular with students and faculty alike. This spring, we were bringing in celebrated author Damon Von Tussel.

The chancellor cleared his throat. "Seems like an actively participating committee member would be up to date on what is happening..." He leaned heavily on "actively participating" so I didn't miss the subtext, which was that he considered me a slacker.

Perfect. When department chair Roland Higgins had passed away, his interim replacement Spencer Bartholomew had suggested I join the planning committee, closing the deal by pointing out that the event was one of the chancellor's pet projects. It would not only put me in contact with the most powerful person at Stonedale but would likely earn me some goodwill, which, after last semester—when the chancellor basically accused me of murdering Roland—was sorely needed.

So far, I didn't seem to be racking up much goodwill at all.

"Most of the planning was done before I started working here," I said evenly, aiming for factual but not apologetic. "I do know Damon is arriving next week."

A smile played over the chancellor's lips. "That's absolutely incorrect. He's already in Colorado, and he is giving a reading in Denver tonight." He raised the piece of paper he held in his slim fingers. "Here is the list of questions we need you to ask him. We'll run the interview in the school paper and on the website on Friday."

There was a long silence while the chancellor waited for me to take the page from him. I didn't. When he pulled his thick brows together, my palms started to sweat inside my thin gloves.

"Unfortunately, I have plans this evening." I knew it was unwise to decline, but I was going to a meeting of the recently formed Stonedale Literary Society, and I was looking forward to our discussion of Toni Morrison's *Beloved*. Plus, I really didn't want to put myself in the position: Von Tussel was known to torment interviewers if he couldn't dodge them altogether. I tried to appease the chancellor with an offer of help. "Would you like me to deliver the questions to Spencer? I'm sure he has someone lined up to take care of this."

"No. I'd like *you* to do it." The man was used to making pronouncements and having them instantly followed. I'd rejected the easiest option for him, which was to hand the questions off to the first person he saw, so now it had become a power thing.

I willed my brain to summon up an effective excuse, stat.

"Is the interview confirmed?" I asked, stalling.

"Of course. We've made arrangements through his agent's office. All you have to do is show up and read from this list." He shook the page he still held in his outstretched hand impatiently. "Do you think you could manage it, Dr. Maclean?" The chancellor tightened his lips.

"Well..."

"I'd certainly appreciate it," he added, with a crisp edge to his tone that I read as a warning.

"All right," I said, resigned. "I'll do it." I took the list from his hand. A flash of triumph crossed his face.

"Oh, how very kind of you," he said, as if I'd volunteered, though we both knew I hadn't. "I'll expect your email tomorrow."

He turned to go, then looked back. "Don't let us down, Dr. Maclean." He held my eyes for a moment before marching up the stairs into Randsworth.

I spun around and plodded home. The last thing I wanted to do was drive to Denver tonight—it was an hour each way—in the snow, in the dark. No time to ponder the complexities of the journey, however; I was now on a mission to retrieve answers from a notoriously reticent author who would almost certainly refuse my efforts to interview him.

Several hours later, I was standing in front of The Savoy. One of

Denver's newest venues in the Art District along Santa Fe Drive, it had been transformed from a dilapidated auditorium into a dazzling Art Deco masterpiece. I paused at the black-and-white poster of Damon Von Tussel out front, all barrel-chested and bearded with his arms crossed in a serious pose, likely cultivating the frequently mentioned similarities to Ernest Hemingway, both physically and verbally. Damon's first book had a strong minimalist style but a dizzyingly fragmented structure; "Hemingway in a blender," some critic had called it.

Inside the theater, I took a minute to appreciate the bold geometric designs and soaring ceiling before locating agent Tally Bendel down by the stage. She denied knowing anything about an interview. Linear in a black tunic, miniskirt, and boots, she appeared almost translucent beneath her overly processed blonde hair, aside from a slash of deep crimson lips. Her black-rimmed eyes were fixed above my head the whole time we spoke. I fought the urge to jump into her line of sight.

Even though I'd explained that the chancellor wanted to generate positive publicity for Damon's upcoming visit to Stonedale, she shook her head and said, "Sorry, doll—my assistant must have forgotten to tell me. In any case, Damon's not in the right mindset. You're better off sending me the questions, and I'll try to get him to answer them soon."

I knew a brush-off when I heard one, though I took the pink neon business card she dangled in front of me just in case.

Plan B was to try my luck backstage, as soon as I could get past security in front of the stage door on the left. All I needed was someone to leave the doorway unattended briefly. We had an hour to go until the reading started, so I took a front-row seat and watched the parade of muscles, all wearing black turtlenecks, cargo pants, and earpieces, guarding the door: one hulk replaced the next every ten minutes or so. I remained poised and ready to strike. For the thousandth time, I reached into my bag to make sure the questions were still there. Once I'd confirmed they were safe, I formulated Plan C. If I couldn't get in to see Damon *before* the reading, then afterwards I would need to sprint backstage, find the author, and throw myself on his mercy. And even if Von Tussel wouldn't answer my questions, I hoped that emphasizing our enthusiasm about the upcoming visit might persuade him to say something—anything—we could use in print.

The chancellor had made it clear that failure was not an option.

I opened the program, which had been thrust though the glass window of the box office with my ticket. It explained that Damon Von Tussel had been a wunderkind of sorts, publishing a critically celebrated novel, *The Medusa Variation*, while in his twenties. The novel was about a young wounded soldier who takes a position as secretary to a crusty old retired colonel writing his memoirs. The soldier helps the colonel go through a lifetime of material—letters, diaries, military paperwork, news clippings, and more; their resulting conversations attempted to make sense of war but inevitably failed. Eventually the colonel commits suicide and the young soldier promises to share his story with the world.

The novel struck a chord with those haunted by Vietnam, became an instant bestseller, and won him numerous awards. Academics were intrigued by the philosophical premise as well as the novel's metafictional structure, which constructed a memoir through myriad textual fragments, and scholars began churning out a veritable cornucopia of work on Von Tussel's book. After several decades of silence, he had recently stunned the literary world by producing a controversial array of prose pieces. The book, *In Medias Res*, was comprised of stories without beginnings or ends, which he called "irrelevant for the new millennium" in a round of interviews showcasing his abrasive and grandiose personality. None of the characters were named, he explained further, in order to allow the reader to "imagine their own protagonist." Devotees had even gone so far as to claim that he had created a new genre, the "medion."

The program *didn't* reprise the rumors that although Von Tussel had been offered faculty positions by all of the best creative writing programs, his classes were always taught by others. Von Tussel had never shown up on campus to fulfill a single teaching obligation. Accordingly, the educational gigs dried up. For years he had been a recluse, holed up in a Tribeca loft in New York City, so everyone was shocked when Damon emerged to publicize *In Medias Res*. There was also no hint at the fact that Damon had begun to act out during his year-long book tour, something I wasn't sure the chancellor was aware of. While many events went off without a hitch and audiences raved about his charming performances, other reports depicted him sneering at interviewers, turning belligerent with fans, cutting readings short, or not showing up at all. There were those who delighted in reporting on social media which Damon Von Tussel had appeared in their reading—#angelDVT or #devilDVT. Such attendees were more fascinated by the potential behavioral issues than the literary ones. His unpredictability only contributed to his mystique.

I was not much of a fan, but here I was, plotting ways to get close to him like a groupie. The things you must do in the hopes of getting tenure.

I waited, checking the stage door incessantly until it was time for Damon Von Tussel to take the stage. A slender man in a dark suit punctuated by a green bow tie meandered through a gushing introduction, his hands shaking so hard that he dropped his index cards and had to scoop them up from the stage. I suspected the spill brought us to the end much more quickly than we might otherwise have dared hope for.

"Without further ado," he said when he stood up, "the amazing Damon Von Tussel."

The author strode onto the stage, waving energetically. He set his book down with a thud on the black lectern and loosened the tie he wore with his blue suit.

"Good evening," he said into the microphone. His voice was low and raspy, advertising years of whiskey and cigars. "Thanks for that generous introduction," he said, glancing back into the wings. "Far better than I deserve." He gazed out into the audience, turning his head slowly to take in the whole crowd and smiled. "And thank you, kind folks, for coming out on this snowy evening. I know it wasn't the easiest trek to make, and I appreciate you being here."

Looked like enchanting Damon was in the house tonight. I could practically feel the #angelDVT tweets blossoming out in cyberspace.

"Here's something from my latest book, *In Medias Res*," he said, then donned a pair of glasses—an exact duplication of Papa Hemingway's, if I wasn't mistaken—and opened the book.

The stage lights were lowered except for the circle of light around Von Tussel's broad, muscular figure. Velvet curtains hung motionless in the background. There was nowhere to look but at him. He read slowly from the open book in his left hand. The right hand stroked his white beard from time to time, but otherwise, he was still. The energy swelling and filling the room arose from only his words.

I had to admit, he had enormous charisma.

He had us right where he wanted us. The audience actively responded to his words throughout—laughing at the humorous parts, gasping at the shocking parts—and rewarded him with loud applause when his final story came to a close. He nodded and set the book down on the lectern. As the noise subsided, he removed his glasses and rubbed his eyes for a moment, then looked expectantly out into the darkness.

The jittery man with the bow tie hurried back onstage to pump Damon's hand. He said a few words to him privately before stepping up to the microphone. "Thank you for a stellar reading," he enthused to the author before addressing the crowd. "Mr. Von Tussel will now take questions from the audience."

We all waited as people made their way down the row and lined up behind the microphone which had been placed in the aisle by an unobtrusive staff member.

A short man in a plaid sport coat and fedora smiled widely at the author. "Congratulations, Mr. Von Tussel, on your new book. I loved it."

Damon inclined his head in thanks.

"I'm wondering why there were so many years between *The Medusa Variation* and *In Medias Res.*"

The author shrugged. "Many people have asked me that. All I can say is the muse works in mysterious ways."

A ripple of laughter cut through the room despite Damon's somewhat dismissive tone.

"But what were you *doing* for all of those years?"

Damon glared at him. "Living," he said, curtly. "How about you?"

The questioner timidly thanked him, and the person in line behind him took his place. I tuned out for the next few questions, checking the doorway to backstage again. Still guarded. Those guys were good. When I finally turned my attention back to Damon, a petite redhead in a navy coat asked something about the idea for the book.

Damon threw his hands into the air and sighed. He leaned into the microphone and barked, "I've answered these questions a thousand times. Do an internet search, for God's sakes. Ask me something *meaningful!*"

The woman, clearly about to cry, began apologizing, but he held up his hand, cutting her off. "Forget it." He whirled around, scraping the book off of the lectern with a jerky movement and charging offstage.

The room fell silent for a moment, then murmurs began to swell into excited commotion. It was clear the author wasn't coming back. People stood to leave.

I glanced over at the stage door, where the security guy had a hand over his earpiece and was listening intently. He abruptly turned and went backstage.

Grabbing my coat and bag, I followed him down the short hallway, passing a small shadowy niche on the left side, probably intended for short-term prop storage. Perfect. I slid into it and glanced around the area.

To the right, in a long rectangular space, individuals were

speaking animatedly with each other or talking into cell phones. Damon strode through the crowd, cutting a clean swath right down the middle as people moved out of his way, and entered a room at the end of the corridor. He slammed the door. A handful of people followed, as if pulled along in his wake, and someone banged on the door until a roar emerged, telling them to leave him alone. Tally Bendel squeezed her way to the front and turned around to face the people standing there.

"Let's give Mr. Von Tussel a break, shall we? I'll see if he can talk to you later, but for now, please give him some space. Help yourself to a coffee on your way out." She gestured toward the area on the right. "It's by the far wall."

Slowly, the others did as she asked. She knocked on the door again, identifying herself. The door cracked open slightly. She spoke through the opening in a low voice. I couldn't hear what she was saying, but after a minute, the door slammed again, and Tally left.

This was my chance. I moved quickly down the corridor until I was in front of the door. I cupped my hand and listened for a second, but I couldn't hear anything. I knocked gently. There was no answer. I twisted the door handle, but it was locked. There was nothing else to do but return to the niche and try again later.

One by one, Damon's agent spoke to some lingerers in the main area, and they left. When it was down to Tally and Mr. Bow Tie, they returned to the room where the author had sequestered himself. She called out to him. There was no answer.

The man called out as well, with the same result.

"Can't you just unlock it?" Tally asked him, placing her hand on his forearm.

He removed a large set of keys from his pocket and sorted through them. "Are you sure?" he asked, looking nervous. Maybe his jitteriness wasn't natural but had been born from earlier encounters with Damon.

She nodded firmly. "He needs me."

He slid a key into the lock and turned the handle. Tally flew into the room, emerging a moment later with a confused expression. She said something I couldn't hear, then they both hurried inside.

I moved to the doorway and peered around the two of them. The room was empty.

Damon Von Tussel had vanished.

Chapter 2

The next day as I made my way across campus, I heard Calista James shouting from somewhere behind me. "Lila! Wait up."

I turned to face my cousin, who was also my colleague; she was bundled up in a dark coat and a scarlet batik-printed scarf. Her gray eyes sparkled beneath the matching hat pulled low over her forehead.

"Did you see Spencer's email?" She tugged at my sleeve to get me moving across the circular expanse at the center of campus known as "the green."

"No. What's going on?" I started to reach for my phone but thought better of it. The sidewalks were icy, and I probably needed to keep my attention focused on not falling—which was harder than it might be ordinarily, given that Calista was practically running. I cautiously increased my speed and followed her to Crandall Hall.

"The chancellor is coming to our emergency meeting today."

"Um..." I swallowed hard.

"It'll be okay," she said. "You did your best."

I did not think the chancellor would agree with her. I had tossed and turned all night, finally rising with dread to call the chancellor and confess I hadn't been able to get the interview. Lucky for me, he'd been out of the office, and his executive assistant had taken the message. I'd hoped that would be the end of it.

As we climbed the marble stairs to the third floor where the English department was housed, she gave me a quick glance. "You're not thinking about Roland, are you?" The last time I'd walked into the first meeting of the semester, I had found our colleague murdered.

"Yes. But we're already three minutes late, so we won't be the first ones there today. If there's anything to be discovered, it won't be by us."

"Good." Calista said. "Let's never be the first ones to arrive."

We entered the arched doorway of the department library and slipped into two of the remaining empty seats at the cherry conference table. The room had been freshly carpeted, painted, and decorated after the "unfortunate incident," as Spencer called Roland's demise. I sank into one of the black leather chairs and took out a legal pad and a pen.

Spencer gave us a kind smile from the head of the table as he rolled up his sleeves. The gray-haired man was the type who brought his suit jacket everywhere but left it on the back of his chair unless formality was called for. He was known for his colorful suspenders—today's were yellow, providing a lively contrast to his perfectly pressed white button-down shirt and charcoal trousers. While Spencer's overall demeanor was gentle, he retained a quiet and effective power, so when he held up his hand, the side conversations halted immediately.

"Let's begin, shall we? I'd like to thank the chancellor for joining us today." He smiled at the man next to him, who dipped his head. "It appears that Mr. Von Tussel is, ah, unavailable. This morning, his agent confirmed that the rest of his appearances have been cancelled." He sliced his hand through the air. "Across the board."

"Including ours." The chancellor frowned.

Spencer nodded. "There were only two appearances left, but yes, including ours."

"Is Damon okay?" Calista asked.

"I don't know the answer to that, unfortunately," Spencer replied in a somber tone. "No one knows where he is."

We all took that in.

"I hope we hear good news on that front very soon," he

continued. "And as much as it pains me to turn our attention to business so immediately in light of the circumstances, we must talk about Arts Week. As you know, the event does a great deal to promote the university. We've already advertised this year's events in everything from the alumni magazine to academic journals. Thus, it will take place as planned next week, and we need to make arrangements for a replacement speaker in a hurry. The chancellor is here today to help us sort through possibilities."

It was rare for the chancellor to venture below deck, so to speak; he preferred to conduct business from the well-appointed confines of his office whenever possible. As one would. He must be under some pressure from the board of trustees to make this event a success.

"Oh, I know," said Calista, waving her hand. "How about Ellora Delgado, the performance artist? She has a new installation at the Denver Art Museum that is to die for, and she's part of a fantastic slam poetry team."

The chancellor stared at Calista, raising his eyebrows slightly, and gave Spencer a pointed look.

Norton Smythe, a man in a cashmere turtleneck who possessed the world's worst comb-over, seized the chance to agree with the chancellor. "Might I suggest we select someone who is much more well-known? I don't think we should consider just anyone because we have a gap to fill." I wasn't surprised that Norton had jumped in after my cousin spoke. He'd tried to put more than a few obstacles in the way of her current tenure bid.

"It's true that we are committed to writers of quality," said Nate Clayton, acknowledging common ground like any effective rhetorician. He had a slender rock climber's build and longish brown hair that retained its highlights from the sun even in the depth of winter because he was an avid skier. "But we also want the students and the wider public to be interested, to sell the most tickets, don't we? In which case, I have to say, Ellora sounds fascinating."

"The students would love her." Calista pushed back her

platinum bobbed hair as she spoke and smiled brightly at the chancellor.

"I think she sounds great." I supported my cousin's suggestion and tacked on a smile as well, following her lead.

"I'm intrigued by Ellora," said Spencer, "and we may need to go with someone local because of our tight turnaround, but let's make a quick list of possible replacements and consider them together."

Over the next half hour, a list of authors to invite was brainstormed and debated. No one mentioned cost, but authors of stature were not inexpensive—and the events began mere days from now. I couldn't fathom how we were going to pull this off. And if this event failed, the chancellor would not only be furious, but he might also pull funding for future events.

"This is troubling," said the chancellor, pursing his lips.

Panicked glances ricocheted around the room. The chancellor usually preferred to indicate his positions through an elaborate set of nonverbal cues in meetings. A heavy sigh from the chancellor meant a pause in the conversation was warranted, readjustment of his water glass indicated that topics should be changed hastily, and a toss of his pen on a legal pad was enough to call for the immediate end of any meeting. The professors who had been here longer were accustomed to making valiant attempts to interpret situations and respond appropriately without earning the chancellor's wrath. Straightforward disapproval was almost unheard of.

Code red, people.

Francisco de Francisco, a handsome African-American man I'd met only recently, cleared his throat. He had blue eyes that matched his denim shirt and a dusting of gray around his temples. He adjusted his glasses, then his bolo tie, which featured a sterling silver animal head with horns, before speaking. "Let's not give up on Von Tussel yet. We've done so much preparation for his visit. Could we wait a few days before we cancel everything?"

Spencer looked doubtful but asked us to go over the event particulars before we made a decision.

"All the preliminary paperwork is in order," said Norton, preening slightly at the opportunity to announce a job well done. "Hotel accommodations have been taken care of as well."

"And I have copies of all the planning materials for you," came a lilting voice from the doorway. The chancellor beamed in the direction of the Grace Kelly lookalike clasping a thick folder to her chest, not seeming at all perturbed at her late arrival. Dang. I hoped perhaps Simone Raleigh had left at the end of last term. Wishes couldn't always come true. She moved gracefully into the room and offered Spencer the photocopies. Before I spiraled too far into despair at the thought of having to deal with my nemesis again, the discussion continued.

"The website is already promoting Arts Week," added Nate. "Though we'll need to make some changes if we have a new speaker."

"And I've made the arrangements for the scholarly panel," Francisco declared.

"What scholarly panel?" the chancellor snapped.

"The one Roland approved last summer before I went on sabbatical," Francisco said, his voice rising. Stonedale gave tenure-track candidates one semester to work on their publications before going up for tenure, which was an uncommon practice but not unheard of. "I sent you all an email back in the fall."

"Hmm," said Spencer, flipping through pages on the table in front of him. "I don't remember that."

The rest of the committee members were shaking their heads too.

I met Calista's eyes. She shrugged almost imperceptibly.

"I didn't hear about it either." The chancellor scowled at Francisco.

Francisco didn't look away. "It's a done deal," he said firmly.

Norton interrupted by waving his beloved antique pipe frantically. "What Francisco means to say is that now would be a good time to finalize the details for the panel, if we are all in agreement. And may I say how overjoyed we are to have you with us today, Chancellor Wellington? We know you are a very busy man."

The display of sycophancy seemed to provide an effective antidote to Francisco's conduct, and the tension in the room dissipated.

Francisco leaned back in his chair, glowering.

"Would you please give us more details?" Calista asked him. "I think it sounds wonderful."

"Delighted to. As you all know, I'm writing a book on Damon. Also, I'm the president of the Von Tussel Society," he said proudly. "We formed officially at last year's Modern Language Association conference." He paused, as if waiting for applause but, not receiving any, plunged onward. "Roland agreed that adding a scholarly panel to the events was an excellent idea, so I sent out a call for papers and organized one. We just need to finalize the day and time."

There was silence around the table.

"The scholars have already bought their plane tickets," Francisco added. "It wouldn't reflect well on the university if we just cancelled on them. In fact, even if we don't end up with Damon here, we should host the panel anyway as a scholarly event."

"Are *you* on the panel?" Norton asked pointedly.

"Yes, but the others are from around the country," Francisco replied, unfazed by Norton's attempt to call out his stake in the matter. "So it has national reach."

"What does Tolliver Ingersoll think about this?" the chancellor asked abruptly. We all looked around the room for our absent committee member as if he might pop up from behind a bookshelf. Someone claimed Tolliver was busy moving to a new home. Someone else said he had already moved last year. A long conversation ensued, during which various theories of his whereabouts were explored, culminating in the realization that no one had any idea where our playwright in residence might actually be residing.

"It really will be spectacular," said Francisco, still selling. "Damon's work is some of the most exciting contemporary writing around, and the scholars on the panel are first-rate." I could tell he included himself in the assessment.

"We have to be careful about overextending," said Norton. "We don't want to turn it into a mini-conference. What is the current schedule of events?"

Spencer rustled through the stack of papers before him, then removed one page and consulted it. "The Pennington Library display of *The Medusa Variation* manuscript will be unveiled on Monday. Our speaker will arrive on Tuesday. Wednesday will be a free day—we've found that guests not used to the elevation benefit from having time to acclimate. A dinner party will kick things off officially on Thursday night. Damon will be expected to teach a workshop on Friday for our students. His reading is scheduled for Saturday evening, to be followed by a book signing. On Sunday, he will attend a reception in his honor at the chancellor's house."

"So we could do the panel Thursday afternoon," said Francisco decisively.

Norton raised his pipe again, wiggling it slightly, his signature gesture. "I'm still concerned about overloading the schedule. Von Tussel, should he manifest himself, is already committed to several events."

Francisco rolled his eyes. "But Damon wouldn't have to be there. It would be optional."

The frown on Norton's face deepened. "I didn't mean only for Von Tussel. I meant for everyone."

"What's the problem?" retorted Francisco. "People can go to the panel if they want and skip it if they don't."

"Will the panel be the only additional activity?" asked Norton, sternly.

"Yes," said Francisco. "Unless someone wants to take it upon themselves to do something." He made it sound as though no one else ever lifted a finger around here.

"Shall we vote on it?" Norton asked, seeming to taking the high road but actually complicating the issue, as we didn't really need to vote on it, as far as I could tell.

"Show of hands," said Francisco, not backing down.

Everyone but Norton, who abstained to register protest without taking an overt stand, voted yes.

The panel was scheduled for Thursday, and we moved on to confirmation of the facility reservations, catering, and all the other hospitality-related issues. I was asked if I wanted to personally escort the author around from event to event, to which I replied—in a flash of inspiration, if I do say so myself—that it might be a better idea to invite some of our students to accompany him, which would give them a chance to talk to a famous writer.

It appeared we had most of the bases covered for the visit, except for actually having a visitor.

"In the unlikely event that we locate Mr. Von Tussel in the next forty-eight hours," the chancellor gave Francisco a long look, "how do we convince him to show up without fail? We must be able to rely on his attendance." He tapped his fingers on the desk lightly.

I heard myself grasp at an enormously unlikely straw. "What if we increase the honorarium we're offering him?"

Francisco took up the baton. "Would you be willing to double the amount, Chancellor?"

After a long pause, the chancellor dipped his chin in affirmation.

"That would probably convince him," Calista said. "Don't you think, Lila?"

I shrugged. "Worth a try."

"Why are you asking *her*?" Francisco demanded, clearly trying to reinstate his authority as The Damon Expert.

"Because she knows him!" Calista exclaimed.

Oh, crap.

When every head in the room turned in my direction, I straightened up in my chair and smiled. Only because that's what was expected. What I really wanted to do was summon a handy puff of smoke into which I could disappear from this conversation.

Francisco was staring at me intently. "Think you could have mentioned this before?"

My cheeks flamed as I shot Calista a reproving look. "I don't know him. Not really. We've met a few times."

"How? Where?" I was fixed in Francisco's burning gaze, with no chance of escape.

Calista answered for me, "Her mother dated him last spring."

My cousin had already been out here in Stonedale teaching, so she'd never met Damon in person, but she had been fascinated by the relationship, following it faithfully across social media. Also, I suspected Calista spoke to my mother on the phone more than I did. We'd all been very close since Calista came to live with us at ten years old when her parents passed away. She felt more like a sister than a cousin, really.

"Hmmm," Francisco replied. "And who is your mother?"

"Violet O." It seemed as though she was always coming up in conversations. Then again, my mother was a public figure, and as far back as I could remember, people wanted to know about her or, more commonly, to get close enough to me to get to know her.

"Ah, yes. A very talented artist indeed," Francisco said.

"Someday you're going to have to tell me everything there is to know about your mother," Nate whispered from the chair next to me. "I am most intrigued."

I waved him off and shook my head.

"Ve haf vays of makink you talk," Nate added, waggling his eyebrows. I stifled a giggle.

Francisco looked thoughtful. "Would you ask your mother to speak to him on our behalf? Make our case?"

"Wouldn't it be better coming from the chancellor?" I ventured hopefully, not daring to look at the chancellor when I said it.

"Look," Francisco said, not giving him an opportunity to respond. "Damon is extremely difficult to track down in the best of circumstances. If your mother knows how to contact him directly, we should go that route."

I became aware of a strange energy in the room, like people were holding their breaths waiting for a response. Their heads swiveled between Francisco and me as if they were watching a fast-paced tennis match. Although he was an assistant professor, on the lowest rung of the hierarchy like I was, he already exuded an unmistakable aura of power. I wasn't sure where it came from. Perhaps he was naturally confident. Or just plain arrogant. In any case, I wasn't about to let him boss me around.

As I was deciding how to respond, the chancellor spoke. "The university would be most grateful, Dr. Maclean."

Well, that clinched it.

"I would be happy to ask her," I lied, the very picture of the cooperative tenure-track candidate.

Across the table, Simone smirked, clearly pleased I'd been obligated to do something I didn't want to do, while Francisco glared, apparently annoyed that I was a few degrees of separation closer to "his" author than he was.

Ah, colleagues.

Calista came into my office as I was packing up to go home. Nate soon followed from his office next door—we had become fast friends last term, and he went out of his way to keep me entertained.

"Does anyone know what's going on with Damon?" Calista wandered over to my overflowing bookshelves. "I mean, after you saw him, Lila." I'd called her last night on the way back to Denver.

"I'm looking online right now," Nate said, scrolling through things on his cell phone screen as he sat in the chair next to my desk. "Tell me what happened."

I closed the flap of my satchel and leaned against the desk. "He gave a superb reading, then he tore off the stage during the question-and-answer part."

"It's so strange that he would bail during a Q&A," Calista said. "If I had a book tour, I'd be thrilled to talk to the audience."

"He didn't sign any books?" Nate asked, still looking at his screen.

"No," I said.

"Aren't sales important?"

"You'd think so."

Calista pulled a thick anthology from my shelf and flipped several pages, then returned the book to its place. "Lil, was he openly disrespectful to the people asking questions?"

"I'd say so. One woman was practically in tears."

"So unprofessional," she said, shaking her head. "You might even say churlish."

"Well, he can be ornery in general," I said.

Nate looked up from his phone. "There's no change to the book tour listing on the publisher's page. Maybe they haven't updated it though."

"Nothing in the news?" Calista asked.

"No, but it hasn't even been a day yet—there's a lag before you can claim that someone is a missing person," Nate told her.

"But what if he was kidnapped?" I asked.

Calista nodded. "I thought about that too."

"I don't know," Nate said. "He seems pretty capable of taking care of himself. Didn't he used to be a boxer back in the day?"

"Still," Calista said, "Someone could have waited for him in his dressing room and chloroformed him—"

"Or clocked him with something heavy," Nate interjected.

"—then they could just drag him away."

I shook my head. "There was a crowd of people right outside his dressing room door. No one could have done that without being seen."

"Maybe there was another exit." Nate looked thoughtful.

"Yes, a second door. Or," Calista said, her voice rising, "maybe there were three or four people waiting for him, and after they knocked him out somehow, they tied him up and passed him through the window into the alley, where they had a van waiting."

We stared at her.

A loud knock on the wall next to my door startled us all. Francisco poked his head into my office.

"You scared me, man," said Nate.

"Me too," Calista added.

"Sorry," Francisco said, not sounding sorry at all. He jabbed his chin at me, the way high school jocks do when they acknowledge each other's presence. "You're on it, right? Von Tussel?"

"Yes," I said. "I'll call my mother tonight."

"You don't look much like her," he said, staring at me. "Isn't she a redhead?"

"Yes." People were always pointing out that my dark wavy hair was unlike my mother's. As if it were unheard of for parents and children to have different colored hair. Not to mention the infinite color options available at salons.

"Hey, my mom—Aunt Vi's twin—had red hair too," Calista protested. "And I'm blonde. It can happen."

"Well, you're blonde *now*..." I said, unable to resist teasing my cousin.

She made a face at me. "It's been so long that I almost forgot I once was a brunette like you."

"Your secret is safe with me," I said, putting my hand over my heart.

"Apparently, it's not," she said, in mock outrage.

"I mean from now on it will be. Now that I know it's a secret."

"Gee, thanks."

Francisco leaned against the open door and crossed his arms over his chest, seeming both amused and annoyed by our exchange. "I still can't believe Damon dated your aunt."

Calista turned to him. "You honestly don't remember? Aunt Vi and Damon were in all the magazines."

"And by 'all the magazines,' do you mean *People*?"

Well, that wouldn't do. I came to Calista's aid. "And *Vanity Fair* and *ArtNews*. Their partnership was documented at all the events they attended together."

"Whatever. Will you text me the instant you hear something?" Francisco reached out his hand in front of me, palm up.

I stared at it.

"Give me your phone and I'll add my number," he said impatiently.

"How about you tell me your number and I'll type it in myself?" I countered, pulling out my cell.

Irritation crossed his face, but he didn't say anything until I had created a new profile for him and poised my fingers over the screen. He gave me the information.

"What were you all whispering about, anyway?" he asked, with a slight sneer. "Got a secret?"

"We were talking about Von Tussel," Nate told him.

"Yeah," Francisco said, drumming his fingers against the doorframe. "I'm sure he's fine. And we need to get him here." He stared at me. "It's all up to you now, Lila."

No one said anything, and after a moment, he left.

Chapter 3

"What's the deal with Francisco?" I asked Nate as we headed home through the snow, our breaths leaving little puffs behind us like steam from a train.

"What do you mean?"

"He's an assistant professor, right?" I buried my chin into the scarf wrapped around my neck. My face was beginning to sting, and my mouth was resisting movement in that exaggerated way created by intense cold.

"Yes."

"Then why doesn't he..." I searched for words. It was one thing to admit to yourself that you were willing to play meek and unassuming as befits junior faculty in the pursuit of tenure, but it was quite another to confess it out loud to a colleague. I darted a glance at Nate, who took pity on me.

"Grovel and stoop like the rest of us?" He grinned.

"Exactly. I mean, he didn't really do anything out of order, but he just had an air about him which seemed..."

"Overconfident?" Nate suggested.

"Okay, let's go with that. Is there a reason he isn't showing...er..."

"Proper humility?"

"Yes. And I appreciate how you know exactly what I mean before I even get to the end of the sentence."

Nate laughed. "I'm just very in tune with wanting tenure. I like having a job."

"I wish I could stop thinking about it. It's down the road, lurking. Like a warrior, I will have to battle. Or a—"

"Monster?"

"Exactly."

"I know how you feel, Lila, but you cannot live every day fearing tenure. I mean, many of us secretly think about it far more than we should, of course, but you have to at least try to push away the anxiety until you come face to face with it. Otherwise, you'll go *mad*." He kicked at a pile of snow.

"I love how you said 'mad' instead of 'crazy.' It's far more literary."

He halted at the corner of Haven Street, where my rented bungalow was located, and University Boulevard, home to his apartment on the second floor of a shabby but comfortable Victorian. "The tenure thing is simple: be professional and do what's expected of you."

"Sure, if you don't count the personality conflicts," I said.

"And all of the political subcurrents," he replied.

"Or the jealousies."

"Or the secret alliances."

"Or any number of factors we know nothing about."

"Yeah," he said, "not counting those."

We looked at each other for a moment and burst out laughing.

"Well, thanks for the advice, Nate. I feel better now." And honestly, I did. "But back to Francisco..."

"Right," he said, as snowflakes coated his watch cap. "He does come across as arrogant, but some academics are like that. And he is really smart. Loves critical theory. He may even be obsessed with it."

Intriguing. "What do you mean?"

"His real name is Robert Franco, but he changed it during graduate school to Francisco de Francisco in order to..." He looked up at the cloudy gray sky for a moment, thinking. "Something about 'mirroring the postmodern condition'...or 'signifying the destabilization of nomenclature'...or something like that."

"Seriously?"

"Seriously. He's a hardcore theory boy."

I laughed. "Theory boy?"

"Sorry. Theory *man*."

"That makes him sound like a superhero."

Nate struck a heroic pose, hand on hips. "Theory Man: here to save the world from the suspension of disbelief!"

I applauded his performance—my gloves muffling the sound—and he bowed gracefully.

"Anyway, Fran's a good guy," he said. "Once you get to know him." He said goodbye and loped down University toward his apartment. I wondered why we had never talked about the fact that he'd kissed me last semester. Just once, but still. I was relieved it hadn't seemed to affect our friendship but was also confused about why we both were acting as if it had never happened.

I trudged the final steps from the icy street to my bungalow. Although I was usually thrilled to be able to walk to work, I was less excited about the prospect when it was ten degrees below zero. Inside, I went straight for the hot cocoa. If I was going to beg my mother to contact her old boyfriend on behalf of my new university, I needed reinforcement. After a few minutes of puttering around in the kitchen, I settled at the small brown oak table with black legs I'd bought for fifty bucks off Craigslist, sipping the cocoa gratefully, savoring the sweet taste and enjoying the warmth of the mug in my hands.

I wasn't sure how my mother would feel about contacting Damon, given their past. Theirs was a tempestuous romance played out in lurid headlines in the many tabloids interested in that sort of thing. The gossip columnists took great delight in heralding every move. They were a high-profile pair and regularly attended events stuffed with paparazzi, so there was really no possibility of privacy—not that either of them would have wanted it. They made their debut as a couple at a New Year's Eve Masquerade Ball. He broke up with her at a hospital fundraising gala, then begged her forgiveness by having a hundred orchids delivered to her Chelsea brownstone. Then she broke up with him at the *La Boheme* after-party, where the two of them had a spectacular fight during which my mother famously threw Damon's cell phone over a balcony into a bubbling fountain three stories below.

I'd met Damon a number of times in New York City while they were dating, but one particular incident stood out in my mind. My mother had been invited to give the keynote address at an upcoming art conference and was in high spirits as she gave me the details over drinks at a bar near her brownstone.

"Are you nervous about giving your speech?" I asked, after she described the weekend ahead.

"Not at all," she said, waving her hand dismissively. "Been there, done that."

A snort came from Damon's chair. After my mother introduced us, he had been checking his phone the entire time while intermittently stroking his neatly trimmed triangular white beard, which prompted me to wonder how much time he had to spend grooming it. He texted furiously, making a variety of grunting sounds as he did so. He was much older than my mother's usual companions—somewhere in his sixties, I'd guess. Although she was in her early fifties—she'd had me when she was only twenty—she tended to date thirty-somethings. And there was no shortage of candidates. My mother had retained every bit of her youthful charisma and, with gentle assistance from her hairstylist, the famous red curls that fell to her waist.

"What is it, my love?" my mother asked, gently touching Damon on the arm. "An upsetting text?"

He looked up, then put his cell on the table. "No. I was just thinking about you, gadding about, talking about your art rather than doing it. What a waste of time."

"Damon!" My mother swatted at him playfully, then turned to me. "He's joking. He likes to tease me."

"No, actually Vi, I'm not. It's absurd how willing you are to squander your gift." He finished his whiskey in one action and slammed it on the table.

My mother stared him down, though she remained composed. "What are you doing, my love? My daughter is here with us. It's not the time for this."

Damon bellowed, "You could be making art. Instead, you are simply talking." He leaned over and enunciated the next few words in an unpleasant blast of his whiskey-scented breath. "Talk, talk, talk. It's a waste of your talent." He paused, then added in a nasty tone, "My love."

She spoke calmly to me. "Lila, would you please excuse us for a few minutes?"

"I should probably go, actually. The dissertation is calling." Which was true, but also I knew my mother could protect herself—in fact, she adored a good row—and I didn't want her to have to hold back with Damon because I was sitting there. On the way out, I hugged my mother slightly harder than usual and wished her good luck at the conference, hoping that would be the last time I ever saw Damon and his facial hair.

That turned out not to be the case. Sadly.

After I finished my cocoa, I dialed my mother's number.

She answered on the first ring, her voice cheery as usual.

"Lila, I'm so glad to hear your voice. I was going to give you a call later this evening to see how the new semester is going."

"Hi, Mom," I said. "How are you?"

She gave me the rundown on her latest project, along with some anecdotes about her best frenemy Daphne Duvall—who had apparently gotten a face lift but told everyone her glow came from a trip to Belize and now everyone was laughing up their sleeves at her. "But enough about me. How are things in Stonedale?"

"Well," I said, "we have a problem."

My mother caught her breath. "Not more dead bodies?"

"No, no."

"Thank God." I allowed her a few minutes of parental fussing rights, then explained that I needed to ask her a favor.

"Of course."

I told her about Damon's disappearance from the reading and our inability to confirm our event. "I hope he's safe," I said. "Have you spoken to him lately?"

"No. We haven't talked at all since our breakup. What does Tally say?" My mother was fond of Damon's agent; they'd bonded instantly last spring.

"She doesn't know where he is, or at least that's what she's telling us."

"That might be true, or she might just be protecting him. You know, doing her job. She gets paid to be a pit bull."

"I understand. And if Damon is truly in trouble, none of this matters. But..." I almost couldn't go on. It seemed heartless to be asking about business when Damon could be tied up in an abandoned warehouse or something right now. Or worse.

"Go on, darling," my mother urged. "What do you need?"

"Well, his cancellation leaves the university in a tight spot, and I've been asked to request that you call Damon on the school's behalf. People are hoping, if it's simply a question of not wanting to attend, that you could persuade him to reconsider. Oh, and the chancellor would like you to mention—again, only if Damon is okay to begin with—that the speaker fee has been doubled."

"Doubled? How generous."

"They're quite serious about getting Damon to Stonedale," I said. "They've been advertising him all over the place."

"I see."

"Not sure why the planning committee wants you to be the one to call him, aside from the fact that you have his direct phone number, but—"

"Oh, I do," said my mother, laughing lightly. "It's because he's a cantankerous buzzard. Everyone else is afraid of him."

"He is intimidating," I agreed.

"Also, he has a terrible habit of not responding when people contact him. I can't tell you how many times I had to apologize for him when we were together. It's a question of manners, really."

"I'm sorry to have to ask. I know you haven't been in touch since you broke up."

"No worries, darling. I'll call him for you. And if I can't get in touch with him, I'll see if I can get Tally to budge."

"Great. It's more important that he's safe—"

"Goes without saying. He probably is...the man does whatever he wants, regardless of how it affects other people. He's probably not even aware that everyone is worrying about him. Or if he is, he doesn't care. Send along the info. And if he won't be your speaker, I certainly would do it."

"Now there's a brilliant plan," I said. "I'll suggest it to the committee if he refuses. Thanks again, Mom. Love you."

"Love you too."

Whew. I could cross that off my list. I probably shouldn't have agreed to be on the committee in the first place, which added far more pressure than I needed, but it was too late to back out.

And now, there were quizzes to be graded.

Chapter 4

"Professors don't always want to do the assigned readings either," I said to the members of my Literary Modernism class—most of whom were slumped in the wooden desks before me. The room was unbearably warm, as if someone had decided that the best way to counter our early February snowstorm was to crank up the heat and melt everything from inside the building. If I weren't standing up to teach, I'd be slumping too.

A few blinks. Some yawns. Effort to connect: denied.

The quizzes I'd graded last night had indicated that a friendly reminder of classroom expectations was warranted, so I lifted the thick anthology from the desk and gave it a shake. "But I promise I will come prepared, and if you do the same, we will have a great deal to talk about."

The students appeared to be waiting for me to say something interesting. I didn't blame them. I shifted gears.

"You know how when you read something, you can get lost in the story so completely that you lose track of time? You pause and it takes a minute to readjust to the real world?"

Some nods.

"Well, a number of these texts won't allow us to relax into the reading. Part of the objective is to keep us *aware* of what we are doing *as* we are doing it." I could feel the tension in the room increase, which was the opposite of what I'd intended. I hurried ahead. "Working through the avant-garde movements can be difficult in general, and there may be moments when you feel lost or confused even if you read a particular piece over and over."

I noted a few stricken looks around the classroom. One woman in a red knit cap looked up from her cell phone and narrowed her eyes. Oops. Stonedale University was a small private school—not Ivy League but prestigious nonetheless—full of students who were accustomed to sailing blithely through their assignments on the S.S. Academic Success. Here I was suggesting that there were choppy waters ahead, and they did not like it one bit. But persevering without certainty was an important aspect of Modernism—and life, for that matter.

"Whenever it gets tough, just keep going. We'll sort it out together, and it will be worth it." I smiled. Reassuringly, I hoped. "So. Let's talk about 'The Love Song of J. Alfred Prufrock.'"

I loved T.S. Eliot's poem for many reasons, and I always looked forward to going beyond the surface of the poem's myriad of complexities into the heart of the matter, which was, in fact, the heart. Or longing, to be more precise.

After a long and lively discussion despite the smothering heat, I reminded them of the short paper due next week and ended the class. As the class was engaged in packing up their backpacks and heading off to the rest of their day, Keandra Lawrence approached my desk, buttoning up a thick coat. It was our first class together, but I was already impressed by her insightful contributions. Her black dreadlocks, which usually fell forward around her face, were pulled back and secured with a red ribbon featuring tiny gothic skulls, which were, I had noticed, all the rage lately.

"Professor? I heard Damon Von Tussel is coming to campus soon and you might need some students to escort him. Do you know who's in charge of that?"

"I'm on the committee, so I can find out for you," I said, realizing it might actually be me. No one had said, exactly, who was in charge. I didn't want to mention that Damon was missing if she hadn't heard about it yet. No need to spread rumors. We'd all know soon enough what was going on.

"Do you like his work?"

Her face lit up. "I love it. My dad is a veteran, and he read *The Medusa Variation* out loud at the dinner table when I was growing up."

I smiled at her. "Nice."

She wrapped a thick scarf around her neck, pausing to carefully extricate her braids. "How about if I email you?"

"Please. I'll email you back as soon as I find out the scoop."

Now I had to figure out how to ask who was doing the organizing without inadvertently getting assigned the task myself. Not that I didn't want to pull my weight in terms of service. I'd be happy to do future tasks. I just wanted to stay as far away from Damon Von Tussel as possible. If he showed up.

After class, I stopped by Norton's office. He was peering through his reading glasses at the computer screen, his head tilted back at an unnatural angle. When he saw me out of the corner of his eye, he ripped the glasses off and tossed them onto his desk next to his pipe.

"Can't see with these things, can't see without them. Absurd." He gestured toward an empty chair. "Sit, sit."

"Thank you, but I just have a quick question."

"Please," he said, his arm still pointing toward the chair. "I want to talk to you."

I sank into the chair, though I didn't remove my coat. After our encounters last semester, all negative, I tried to keep a healthy distance. He was an esteemed Chaucer scholar with a wicked wit and keen mind, judging from the articles I'd read, but I was wary of him.

"You first," he said magnanimously.

"Do you know who is organizing the students for Damon's visit? If he visits..." I held my breath, hoping he wouldn't say it was me.

"Not sure," he said. "What did you think of the meeting, by the way?" As he waited for me to respond, he smoothed the horizontal row of spindly hairs he'd arranged carefully across his skull.

"It was...productive," I said, trying not to stare at his comb-over. I wasn't sure where he was going with this line of questioning.

"Do you think a panel is a good idea?"

Oh. Francisco's panel. "It could be interesting," I said noncommittally.

He studied me, his dark brown eyes unreadable. "Fair enough," he said finally.

As I stood to leave, he added, "By the way, if you are at all interested in tenure, you might want to get started on the Isabella Dare book you mentioned in your interviews."

I whirled back around. "At all interested" in tenure? It was *all* I was interested in, and he knew it. "Pardon?"

"Well, the tenure committee met yesterday to discuss some business, and we also made a calendar listing who would be coming up for tenure and when. It made me think about publications. And how important it is to have them."

My mouth went dry.

"You don't have any yet, right?"

I shook my head. "Just conference presentations."

He gave me a tight smile, patting his pipe, which he was not allowed to smoke inside the building, absently. "Well, then..."

The implication of my impending failure filled the room, making it harder to breathe. I thanked him and raced back toward my office, barreling into Nate just outside my door.

"Whoa," he said. "Who's chasing you?"

I put my finger to my lips, shushing him. He instantly looked both concerned and puzzled.

Managing to fit my shaking key into the lock, I pulled him inside the office and shut the door.

"Norton just completely freaked me out," I said, recounting the conversation for him. "Here I was trying to do like you said and push tenure out of my mind. And now it's right back in my face again." My eyes filled with tears, which happened sometimes when

I was especially frustrated, much to my dismay. "Are they going to be reminding us about it constantly? I don't think I can handle that."

He perched on the edge of my desk, smelling pleasantly of soap, as he always did. "Lila, it's okay. You have years until you have to apply for tenure."

"So why did he mention it to me *today*?"

Nate grabbed a tissue from the box on my bookshelf and handed it to me. I dabbed at my eyes.

"Who knows?" he said. "He may want you to have as much time as possible to work on a project, so he's mentioning it now. He may genuinely want you to succeed."

"Or he may be trying to discourage me by implying that the tenure committee is worried because I haven't published anything yet. And preparing me for the worst."

"That's not likely," he said. "It's only your first year."

"I've only been here one semester," I protested. "I didn't get much research done because I was trying not to get killed!"

He patted my arm. "I know. Look, no one expected you to publish something immediately. And honestly, whatever Norton did mean by it doesn't matter. Look at it this way: he could tell you right now you weren't getting tenure—"

I gasped. "Don't say that out loud!"

"—but it wouldn't mean anything. It's not up to him alone."

"True," I said, calming down.

"There is a lot of time between now and then." He smiled at me. "You'll publish when you're ready. Don't stress."

"Easy for you to say," I sniffled. "You already published a ton of articles and you're almost done with your book."

"One measly article. And maybe no one will want to publish my book. I'm only a year ahead of you, Lila."

I resolved right then and there to finish the book proposal I'd started last fall and worked on over break. It was time to send it into the world. One thing my dissertation director Avery had insisted upon was that I kept publication after graduation in mind as I wrote the project. And thank goodness I had. Now if I could just find a publisher who was interested, which seemed like an impossible dream. But clearly I had to behave as though it wasn't.

After some deep breathing exercises, I was composed enough to tackle some work. I had fallen more than the usual amount behind already.

As soon as I'd settled down at my desk and turned on my laptop, a text arrived from my mother: *Damon said yes.*

My whole body relaxed. That meant that he was alive and well, which was most important. And now we didn't have to scramble for a replacement. I dashed off an email to the planning committee, imagining collective sighs of relief all around. I couldn't wait to hear how my mother's conversation with Damon had gone.

I wasn't surprised she had managed to locate the man the rest of the world was looking for; she was a very determined woman who typically got what she wanted when she put her mind to it.

I'd bet if she were in my shoes, she'd already have managed to get tenure somehow.

As the wise Cervantes said, comparisons are odious.

Returning to the computer, I made my way down the list of emails from students and colleagues. The last one had a name and email address I didn't recognize, but the subject line read "Arts Week." Planning committee member names and emails were on the university web page as contacts, and I'd received quite a few queries asking about various particulars. I clicked on it, ready to dispense whatever information was required and move on to grading.

The email was short but not so sweet: *Cancel Damon Von Tussel or else.*

Seriously? We'd just managed to wrangle the author back onto the schedule and now someone wanted us to cancel?

I checked the email header again. Nothing about the person's name or email service was familiar.

Leaning back in my chair, I stared at the screen. I wasn't sure if this was the kind of thing better filed in the "crank" or "concern" category, so I printed it out and headed toward Spencer's office.

As I passed the faculty mailboxes brimming with flyers and student papers, I greeted Mei Tan, a student who worked part-time in the office. After reading "Two Kinds" in American Lit last term, we'd bonded over our shared admiration of Amy Tan—"No relation," Mei had said to the class, "though I sure hope an agent thinks so when I send out my novel." She was leaning against the wall typing away on her cell phone, her long dark hair shining prettily in the glare of the overhead lights.

I complimented the large rainbow-colored peace sign on her phone case, and she looked up.

"Oh, hey Dr. Maclean. Sorry—I didn't hear you. I'm in the writing zone. Do you need something copied? This is going to take a little while," she said apologetically, indicating the rumbling machine next to her, which was spewing out collated packets of something.

"No, thanks. I'm just here to speak to Dr. Bartholomew, if he's in."

"He is indeed," she said, swerving her pointer finger in a right-this-way gesture toward his office door, the movement releasing a tiny burst of patchouli scent.

"How's your writing going?"

She held up her phone. "I'm writing a poem as we speak."

"What excellent multi-tasking," I said appreciatively, as I moved toward Spencer's office, where I paused to give a little knock on the doorframe and froze.

Mei laughed. "It's totally different, isn't it? Everybody gasps when they see it."

Gone was the suffocating crypt-like decor that Roland had created. The massive mahogany desk still faced the door, but instead of one skeletal chair in front if it, there were two inviting wing chairs positioned atop a lush and elegant carpet. Instead of the mounds of dusty books and papers piled haphazardly on every conceivable surface, there were tidy bookshelves and a few tasteful pieces of art. The light streaming in through the windows was also in direct opposition to the previously overwhelming darkness, and a vase of fresh flowers stood on a side table.

"It looks amazing in here," I said to Spencer.

"Judith did it all, as you probably could have guessed." His suspenders today were the color of aged parchment with small letters looping across the fabric in intriguing ways. They gave the appearance of having been sewn from a manuscript. I wanted to read the printed words but couldn't figure out how to do so without putting my face mere inches from his chest. That would have been awkward for both of us.

"I'm sorry to bother you, Spencer, but I just received a weird email."

"Is it about Damon?" He grimaced as he lifted a page from his desk and held it out to me.

I handed him my email and scanned the one he gave me.

Identical.

Our eyes met, and he sighed. "You know, I'd just seen your email confirming Damon's visit. I thought perhaps our troubles might be over."

I handed him back the paper. He lay both pages on his desk and gazed out the window, deep in thought.

There wasn't anything for me to say. This was way beyond my pay grade.

Finally, he ran a hand over his gray hair and nodded. His usually gentle demeanor was spiked with something steely, though his words remained calm. "I'll call the dean and chancellor right now. We'll look into it, check with the rest of the committee, talk to campus security, and so on." He picked up the phone. "Try not to worry too much. It's probably just someone's idea of a prank."

I certainly hoped that was the case.

I did *not* want to find out what "or else" meant in practice.

Chapter 5

On the walk home, the sound of my boots crunching on the ice was an oddly satisfying companion to the brittle shell of defensive anger I retained not only from the threatening email but also from the exchange with Norton. He had to know that expressing doubt about my ability to produce suitable scholarship was akin to lashing an albatross around my neck. Not that it wasn't there already: I knew what was expected of me. But somehow, I hadn't anticipated anyone mentioning it yet. Was he being cruel? Or kind? I hadn't had a chance to get to know him, though I remained suspicious enough from our brief encounters last term. The truth will out, my mother always said.

I was just passing the steps of Pennington Library when Simone Raleigh emerged through the glass doors. She called my name, waving excitedly with one of her leather gloves, and asked me to wait.

Reluctantly, I did.

"Thanks, Lila. Need a quick word, if you don't mind." I don't know how, but she often made me feel as though she was the hostess of a party and I was a guest who had just barely made the list and should consider myself lucky to be addressed by her though she was taking pains to pretend she thought we were equals.

"Sure. What's up?"

"I just ran into Norton at the reserve desk—he's such a dear, isn't he?" She readjusted the large black Jackie O. sunglasses she wore even though it was overcast. "He told me you asked about organizing the students to help Damon during his visit. I'd be happy to take on the responsibility."

"Great," I said. "I have a volunteer in one of my classes already—I don't know how the word got out but she came up after class and said she was interested."

"Keandra, right?" Simone said, catching me by surprise.

"Yes..."

"She's in my class right after yours and spoke to me about it. She said you were going to email her once you knew, but don't worry about that. I'll take care of it."

"Thanks," I said. I knew better than to allow this sudden burst of helpfulness to affect my existing opinion of Simone—I'd seen her in action before.

"Also, are you free for coffee tomorrow? I'd like to have a little chat."

"I'm not."

She waited for a moment, probably so that I'd provide a reason. I didn't—because my reason was I didn't want to go.

"Another time, then," she said, pulling a long face. "We have some things to...address."

It didn't sound like a "little chat" at all.

"Simone, we don't have to have coffee to"—I added air quotes—"chat. You can say whatever you like right now. You've certainly done that before." I could feel my face flush with anger.

She summoned a faux puzzled look. "I'm sure I don't know what you mean."

"And I'm sure you do." I didn't know why she was pretending we didn't have a history. We had one. We had both begun teaching at Stonedale last fall, but she'd had it in for me from the beginning. Someone had told me her sister had applied for the position I'd landed. That was enough to put me on Simone's hit list, and as she was a close personal friend of the chancellor's, it was especially worrisome. I couldn't bring myself to relax around her, but I wasn't going to let her push me around either.

"Perhaps I'll invite you again another time," she said, still playing the role of society girl who magnanimously ignored the foibles of her unsophisticated country cousin.

I said nothing.

Simone drifted away gracefully down the sidewalk, tossing her teal pashmina over her shoulder. She seemed to glide over the ice without any effort.

My own exit may have involved more stomping.

I curled up on my red chenille sofa with a cup of peppermint tea to prepare my next classes. I'd just finished the first one when my cell rang. It was my mother.

I greeted her as I pushed aside the papers and books on my lap.

"Just wanted to let you know that Damon is fine—he apparently took off through a back door at the reading the other night."

"Why?"

She laughed. "Who knows? The man is a mystery. In any case, right now, he's at a friend's mountain house in Vail."

"Where did you hear this?"

"From Daphne first." Of course. Daphne Duvall was the clearinghouse of New York City gossip. She wrote a popular column for one of the tabloids and knew who was up to what long before the public got wind of it. "And he confirmed it when we spoke. He was, as you'd suspected he would be, interested in the doubled honorarium. I also called Tally, who promised me that she'd get him to Stonedale, even if she has to drive him herself."

"Thank you so much, Mom."

"It was nothing," she said. "I was happy to help."

"Was it strange to talk to Damon?" I asked, genuinely curious.

"No, it was as if not a day had gone by. He said he'd just been thinking about me." Which was no surprise. People were always thinking about my mother.

"How is he doing?"

"Well, I think. He's been doing a lot of publicity for the book, so he has been out and about more than usual. He invited me for a drink when he gets back to the city, actually."

"Are you going?" I held my breath. I did not want Damon back in my mother's life.

"We'll see. It's crunch time now with the show coming up. I'm not sure I can spare a moment until after the opening." She told me about her upcoming installation, which was sure to cause a buzz: "The Siren Song" would move incrementally from ethereal fare, women in flowing white gowns and halos, to models in ripped black leather with glittering wounds.

"I want to visualize the angel/demon dichotomy as a manifestation of how society has victimized but also blamed the female body for that same victimization." She sounded excited.

"Should get some attention," I said.

"Yes, it should," she agreed happily. "I wish you could be there."

"Me too. I'll try to make it to New York during spring break."

"That would be fabulous."

After a few more minutes of conversation, we said our goodbyes and I went back to work.

The next afternoon, I was sitting at a small wooden table at the front window of Scarlett's, my favorite café near campus. A pile of essays waited to be graded before me, but I was sipping my latte and watching the water drip steadily off the striped awning. The sun had come out in full glare this morning, and it was making short work of the frozen landscape, emptying the roofs of their white crowns and reducing snowdrifts to puddles. Colorado wasn't a place for people who appreciated being able to count on the weather. You never knew in the early months of the year whether it was going to be more like winter or spring. But after a week of gray, I was ready for some sun on my face, if only through glass at the moment.

The bells on the door tinkled merrily, and I glanced over. Francisco strode up to the counter to place an order. I quickly grabbed the top essay and pretended to be deep in reading mode. I didn't want another colleague confrontation to ruin my small peaceful moment. Soon after, I felt his presence beside me and had to look up.

"Hello, Lila," he said, his blue eyes boring into mine through his rectangular glasses.

"Hi, Francisco." I didn't look away, sensing it was some kind of alpha thing. Eventually he blinked and asked if he could sit down.

I removed my satchel from the seat next to mine and set it on the floor. He slid into the chair, his navy pea coat smelling faintly of pine.

"I wanted to talk to you about the Von Tussel visit. I've made the arrangements for the panel: we'll have four readers. Each will present for fifteen minutes, then we'll have a half hour of questions."

"Ah," I said. A pretty standard format. I wasn't sure why he was making a point of telling me.

He ran his hand through his short dark hair. "We need a panel moderator though—someone who knows Von Tussel's work. Would you be willing to do it?"

There it was. "Uh," I stalled. I would prefer to be in the audience, safely away from the limelight. I studied the silver around his temples, trying to think of an excuse.

"Since you know him..." His hands made an elegant gesture.

"But I don't know him," I said, emphatically. "My mother does." Why did people keep saying that when I'd made it clear I only met him a few times? Were we academics so desperate to be respected we'd turn any brief encounter into something more? "And I don't know his work," I added, for good measure. "Not really."

Francisco considered my response, then shrugged. "But you are a professor."

I nodded.

He pushed his glasses up. "So you could moderate a panel of scholars, at least. Regardless of topic."

"I suppose so. Theoretically."

He took my words to mean I'd agreed to do it. When I protested, rather loudly, he put his hands up to stop me. "I will consider this a personal favor."

So there was that.

Chapter 6

I spent several hours over the next week doing online research on the panel presenters to get a sense of their backgrounds. Across the board they seemed like active scholars, and I was looking forward to hearing them talk about Damon's work.

Finally, I was able to turn to my Isabella Dare proposal on Saturday. Her writing was engaging and unusual—something like a cross between Agatha Christie and Shirley Jackson—and I hoped to turn my dissertation into a book not only because it was expected for tenure, but also because I believed Dare deserved to be read and studied by others. Last fall, my colleague Willa Hartwell had vigorously encouraged me to try and publish Isabella's books as well as my own critical study of them. I had long imagined doing that very thing, but for her to show such excitement gave me hope it might actually be possible. Of course, I didn't know the first thing about publishing a book—neither my own critical study nor a scholarly edition of Isabella's mysteries. But I'd researched how to write a proposal online and, now that Norton had lit a fire beneath me, was going to take the next step.

I picked up the closest of the three novels she'd written. As always, when I began reading her work, time slipped away. She had an incredible ability to immerse the reader immediately with her lively voice and suspenseful plots. In the first book of the series, *The Case of the Wandering Spirit*, our plucky protagonist Athena Bolt was charged with investigating a strange urban legend connected to an abandoned mansion outside of New York City. Just as Athena was approaching an attic door which had mysteriously swung open, the phone rang.

Even though I'd already read the book numerous times and knew what was behind the door, I jumped. That's how good at creating suspense Isabella Dare was—one reason I hoped to bring attention to her work.

"Dr. Maclean?" said a perky voice on the other end of the line.

"This is she," I said, bracing myself to reject the inevitable sales call.

"Ruth Barnum here," the voice said. "Head librarian at Pennington. We have received the Damon Von Tussel manuscript and wonder if you'd be able to stop by Sunday and help us with the arrangement of the document for display."

I hesitated, running through the items on my mental to-do list before Monday.

Ruth interpreted my pause correctly. "I know it's probably an imposition, on the weekend and everything, but Dr. Judith Westerly suggested you as a consultant. We just want you to take a quick look and give us a scholarly perspective."

I had no idea what that meant. Presumably, it was a stack of typed pages. What did they want me to do, make sure the pages were lined up correctly? Then again, if Judith had been the one to recommend me, I could hardly refuse. She was my mentor and friend—as well as Spencer's wife. They'd both been very kind to me.

"I'd be happy to help," I said. "When do you need me?"

We made plans for the next morning and disconnected, then I went back to work.

There was ice on the stone steps of Pennington Library, so I ascended carefully. It was extremely quiet on campus, partly because it was a Sunday morning and partly because Ruth had asked me to come two hours before the library opened.

I headed for the employee entrance door on the side, where Ruth had directed me, and rang the buzzer. After a moment, the lock clicked, and I went inside. A petite woman with a fuzzy yellow woolen sweater showcasing a sweet-looking Yorkshire terrier over a long denim skirt came toward me, and we exchanged greetings. Ruth's brown hair was styled in a flip and embellished with a wide orange headband featuring more terriers. I asked the obvious question and was treated to an enthusiastic rendering of Mr. Barkley's adventures at the last Westminster Dog Show. She pulled a plastic accordion of pictures from her skirt pocket and showed off her adorable pup, whom I complimented profusely.

After carefully refolding the photo strip, she pointed at a row of silver hooks along the wall where I could hang my coat. As I unbundled, she said she was glad I was here. I assured her I was happy to help.

"Please follow me," she said, crossing the room and disappearing to the right just outside the door.

We walked through the library, which was silent and lit by only a portion of the overhead lights. At the back of the building, she went through a wooden door marked STAFF ONLY, and we entered an even darker hallway. After a few minutes, she paused next to a spot where light showed through a vertical crack. She fumbled with a key, then unlocked and pulled open two sides of the back of the display case. It was too dim to make out any objects inside the case.

"Here's what we have so far," she said, gesturing. "Could you please go around to the outside and view it as an onlooker would? I'd really like to know, firstly, can you read it clearly enough through the glass? And secondly, should we make more single pages visible? We chose a few from the middle to showcase. And thirdly, are certain pages more appropriate than others?" She shook her head. "This all happened so fast. I'm just not feeling very confident about the choices we've made."

Now I understood why I was here.

"I'll do the curtains and lights when you're standing in front of the case," she continued.

Once I was located in the correct position, the blue curtains slid open and the lights flickered on inside the case, allowing me to scrutinize the display. On the left side of a gorgeous mahogany desk was the manuscript title page in a clear acrylic frame, a black vintage typewriter with a page in the roller, and a neatly stacked pile of typed pages. Several single pages were spread out in an orderly row. It was an engaging writing tableau. On the back wall was a collage of black-and-white pictures of Damon Von Tussel: hunched over a typewriter, shaking hands with someone, sitting at a bus terminal, talking to a group of students, walking in Central Park. I took a closer look at the single pages, skimming them, and recognized an important scene in the book, when the colonel and the young writer argue over documents so intensely that it results in a fistfight followed by emotional confessions on both sides. It had received homage from numerous writers who followed.

I gave Ruth the thumbs-up through the glass and saw relief cross her face. She closed the curtains and came out to join me.

"Looks great, Ruth," I said. "Honestly, you couldn't have picked a better scene to showcase. This is a famous one."

"Whew," she said, drawing her hand across her forehead. "Good to know. Don't tell anyone, but I haven't even read this book."

"How did you select the pages?"

"My son recommended the scene. He's an English major at UCLA. They read *The Medusa Variation* in one of his classes."

I nodded.

"I trust him, of course, but...well, the chancellor himself made the request for this display, so I thought a second opinion might be in order."

"It all looks wonderful," I said. "Where did you get the pictures?"

"The publisher sent them," she said. "They were delivered with the manuscript, in one box. By armed guard."

"Armed guard?" I knew art pieces could travel with such protection, but I hadn't heard about manuscripts receiving the same treatment before. Or had I? Jack Kerouac's *On the Road* scrolls perhaps? I knew they were bought for several million dollars and had been shown in various libraries and museums, but I had no idea how they were transported from one location to the next.

"Pretty intense guys too, I must say. They made me uncomfortable," she admitted.

"Why?"

Ruth put a finger to her lips as she thought. "It was quite formal and serious. We signed document after document. First time we've ever had to do something like this. Though maybe it was the guns they were wearing that made me nervous." She brightened. "In any case, we're all excited."

"Can I help with anything else?"

"No, this is it. Thanks so much, Dr. Maclean."

"Lila, please," I said.

She smiled at me. "Lila. Really appreciate your assistance. Can you find your way back to your coat?"

"Yes," I said, turning to go, then pausing. "When will this be open to the public?"

"Tomorrow morning," she said happily. "We have a ceremony planned for ten thirty. You should come."

"I'll try," I assured her. "Thanks for the invitation." I started back across the library.

"Invite everyone," she called out. "It would be great to have a crowd."

My nine a.m. American Lit survey class ended fifteen minutes before the manuscript unveiling. After I told them about the event, a number of students were eager to attend, so we walked over to Pennington together.

The library was packed. I'd seen the email blast sent out to the entire university, as well as a number of social media announcements, but I hadn't expected the unveiling to be such a draw. The first floor of the library was cordoned off at the halfway point and people filled the rest of the available space, right up to the entrance and exit doors.

The students wandered off, and I claimed a spot next to the circulation desk, appreciating the way sunlight was filtering through the tall pine trees outside and into the full-length windows along the far side.

After a few minutes, Ruth appeared in front of me. Her long red corduroy dress was paired with another terrier-dotted headband. "Come up to the front, Lila," she said. "In exchange for your help. It's the least I can do."

"Oh no," I demurred. "I saw it yesterday. Let everyone else have a peek before I look again."

"Actually, the chancellor wants to have a word," she added meaningfully. That was a direct quote, I knew.

I followed her through the crowd, murmuring apologies for the inconvenience. We got a few annoyed looks, but eventually made it to the front, where the chancellor was terrifying a poor dean from the business school whose name I couldn't remember. The dean was quaking in his highly-polished loafers; I stared at his trembling face with concern. When Ruth said hello, the dean looked so relieved for the interruption that I thought he was going to hug her; instead, he began taking baby steps backwards while thanking the chancellor profusely for listening. When the chancellor turned to face us, the dean spun around and broke into an all-out run for the stairs to the second floor.

I stood up straighter, as I did every time I was in the same room as the chancellor.

He held out his hand, which I shook. It was moist and clammy, but I held off wiping my hand surreptitiously on my pant leg until he looked back toward the curtained display case and made a grand gesture.

"Very pleased," he said. "This is a boon to our school. Good publicity." Good publicity was high on the chancellor's list of desirable outcomes. It tended to translate into money coming in.

"I didn't have anything to do with it," I said.

"Oh, but you did," said Ruth. She was beaming at me. "I very much appreciated your consultation and expertise, Dr. Maclean."

"Lila," I said gently. "Please."

"Almost makes up for last semester," said the chancellor, fixing me with a look. He'd considered it very inconvenient I'd found a dead body in the department library at the beginning of the term. That was bad publicity. The opposite of his favorite thing.

"Oh," I said, mustering up my brightest smile for him. "I'm glad."

"I said *almost*," the chancellor responded. "I've still got my eyes on you." He pointed to his glasses with two fingers and then pointed them at me.

"We won't mention the essential interview that you failed to obtain," he continued.

By which he meant putting it out there between us as if inscribed in neon.

"Chancellor Wellington?" We all turned in the direction of the loud voice beside us. A man in a rumpled tan suit shoved a microphone into the chancellor's face.

The chancellor gave the intruder a tight smile.

The man's lanyard press card identified him as Terrance Brown of *The Stonedale Scout*, our town newspaper. He launched into question mode. The chancellor explained the importance of the manuscript and made some comments about how grateful Stonedale University was to the publisher who had made the display possible.

Terrance began another volley of questions, but the chancellor looked at Ruth, who directed her cheerful gaze in his direction. "Shall we begin?" He took a step away from the reporter, indicating that the interview was over.

Ruth addressed the crowd, her hands clasped in front of her. "Welcome, everyone. We are delighted to have you with us this morning for the unveiling of Damon Von Tussel's manuscript of *The Medusa Variation*, for which the author has won many literary prizes. The library would like to thank Chancellor Wellington for convincing the publisher to share the manuscript with us. Please follow me."

She unhooked the belt of the barrier, which retracted into a small pole on the other side, and moved purposefully across the library floor, past the catalog computer terminals and several rows of tables and chairs filled with students. The crowd surged behind in her wake, chattering excitedly.

We collected in front of the blue-curtained window. The excitement was palpable. One heavily bewhiskered guy in a wool coat next to me was rubbing his hands together briskly, like some old-timey character suffused with private glee. The students were all holding up their cell phones, ready to snap a shot to post on social media. It was an odd juxtaposition, both generationally and visually. But we were all enthusiastic, in our own ways, to be part of this event.

Finally, the moment had come. Ruth raised her hands in front of us, and the crowd fell silent.

"Ladies and gentlemen, I present"—she signaled someone off to the side who spoke into their cell phone, presumably giving the "go" sign—"*The Medusa Variation*!"

The crowd moved forward as the curtains slowly slid backwards to reveal the desk.

It was empty.

Chapter 7

I looked up in confusion and, as luck would have it, met the chancellor's eyes. He narrowed them.

As I processed the fact that the chancellor was somehow displeased with me—again—I was pulled roughly to the right of the display case. Ruth grabbed both of my shoulders and peered into my face.

"What happened?" Her voice was high and squeaky.

"I don't know," I replied. "Was everything there this morning?"

Ruth shrugged. "I didn't even look. We had so much to do to get ready for the crowds—we had to move all the tables and chairs away from the center of the room and put signs up about the exhibit around the building, and..." She fell silent, her eyes still moving rapidly around as if looking for an explanation. Her face was flushed in an unhealthy way.

Time to take charge.

"Ruth," I said firmly, "call Campus Security."

"Not the Stonedale police?"

"You will probably want to call the police too, especially given the value of the manuscript, but start with them."

She nodded, her lips pressed together with new determination. Just as I suspected, she was a take-charge person. She readjusted her terrier headband, pulled out an old-school flip phone, and started pushing buttons.

*   *   *

Around eleven thirty, things were finally calming down. Campus Security had arrived and had begun questioning the people who remained. Most of the crowd offered some variation of "I didn't see anything," which was an unfortunately literal description given the empty desk which they'd been presented with so much flourish.

Ruth, the chancellor, a student with a library staff nametag identifying him as Hamley, and I were waiting at one of the tables off to the side. We did not talk, per instructions, as we filled out our incident reports. I was glad to have something to look at besides the accusing eyes of the chancellor.

I had just completed the form when we were joined by a slender man with straight black hair and a Campus Security patch on the shoulder of his dark uniform. He carried a bike helmet with a mirror attached under one arm and a notepad in his left hand. He placed both carefully on the table top before introducing himself as Officer Heiko. I didn't know the officers rode bikes in the winter. Maybe it was on a case-by-case basis or maybe it was officer preference. Not that it mattered right now. I shook my head to refocus on the conversation at hand.

Officer Heiko asked Hamley why he'd left his post. I hadn't even known there was a guard planned, and I looked at him with interest.

Hamley, with a dismayed expression, shook his blond hair out of his eyes before answering. "I'm really sorry, Ms. Barnum," he said to Ruth. "I had to leave for a minute."

"Whatever for?" the chancellor demanded.

Hamley flushed. "Uh...well...nature called."

The chancellor rolled his eyes.

"It's okay, Hamley," Ruth said soothingly. "I should have done a rotation to give you a break."

After a few more questions, Officer Heiko dismissed Hamley and turned to us.

"Do you trust him, Ms. Barnum?"

"Hamley? Oh heavens, yes. He's my neighbor. I've known him since he was four years old. Was happy to give him a job here at the library when he started at Stonedale. He's been here two years now and is one of our best workers. That's why I asked him to stand guard."

We provided as much information as we could. The chancellor described the arrangements made with the publisher, which turned out to involve almost heroic amounts of persuasion, at least the way he told it. Ruth repeated the story about the armed-guard arrival and mentioned she'd had me come in and take a look on Sunday morning. I corroborated what Ruth said.

"Okay, help me out here," said the officer. His voice was quiet but authoritative. "What was in the case, exactly?"

Ruth identified the manuscript materials and photos on display, and he wrote them down. "Oh, and a vintage typewriter too. But it was only a prop. I don't know why someone would steal that."

The officer made a star by the item on his list. "Everything else in the case was from the publisher?"

She nodded.

"Who had access to the display case this morning?"

"No one," said Ruth. "The curtains and lights are controlled by switches in the hallway. There was no need for anyone to go inside the case. And I had the key, for what it's worth, and it was in my pocket all day."

"Isn't there a master?" asked the chancellor curtly.

"There is a master key in the library vault," Ruth said. "But only the director of the library and I know the combination, and she's out of town. Her daughter had a baby," she said, dimpling sweetly at the thought.

"So the case was left unlocked." The chancellor glared at Ruth.

"Oh no," Ruth said, waving her hand in dismissal. She didn't seem to register the blame shooting out of his eyeballs with white-hot intensity. "I double checked it Sunday night—"

"It doesn't matter," Officer Heiko interrupted softly. "Wasn't opened with a key. Someone broke the lock. You can't tell by looking at it because the doors were closed again and lined up perfectly, but it was drilled into."

Ruth and I stared at each other.

The chancellor made an exasperated sound and pushed his incident form across the table. He rose to stand. "The good news is that the manuscript is insured. The bad news is that it may be lost forever. More bad publicity," he said, glowering at me. "Why do these things always happen when *you're* around, Professor?"

I cast about for a response but came up empty.

Ruth patted my arm.

He shook his head in disgust.

"I have an important meeting," he boomed. "Call me when you have answers." Officer Heiko nodded and the chancellor strode away.

"I have class at noon," I said apologetically—trying to counter the chancellor's abruptness. "Are we done?"

"For now," said the officer. "You've included your contact information on the incident form?"

"Yes," I assured him. "Feel free to call me if you think of anything else."

"That I will, Dr. Maclean. Appreciate your help."

I gathered up my things and hustled across campus—coasting into the classroom as the clock struck twelve. If that could be stretched to mean three minutes after the hour. Shh.

Later that evening, I awoke with a start. I'd been dreaming a shaggy werewolfian creature had cornered me in a classroom after a long chase across campus. The red numbers on my clock radio informed me that it was just after two a.m. I tried to go back to sleep, but the adrenaline shot had propelled me right into awake mode. I'd learned over the years that in such situations, it was better to pull myself out of bed and do some small project; otherwise I'd toss and turn for hours, the anxiety increasing with every passing hour.

Occasionally, it could even trigger a panic attack—a most unpleasant experience.

I'd never had a single panic attack in my life until I decided to pursue a career in academia. Best not to dwell on that fact for too long.

I shuffled out of the room and plopped down on the sofa. Maybe I would watch some TV. When I leaned forward to grab the remote, I came face to face with a mountain of papers on my coffee table. I supposed I could get some grading done; my Modernism students had turned in essays on Zora Neale Hurston today. I pulled the stack toward me and settled in to read and make comments. Several hours later, I could see the light outside my windows beginning to brighten, and I was almost through the stack. The majority of the essays were solid, with engaging ideas, strong claims, and thoughtful evidence from the texts as support.

When I picked up the final essay and began reading, the first paragraph set off warning bells. I couldn't place it, but I had the sense I'd read it before, and the language didn't sound like student writing either. I checked the student's name at the top—Stephanie Barnes. Skimming the rest of the essay only reinforced my suspicions. With a sinking feeling, I went over to my desk and turned on my laptop, then went to start the coffee machine. Time to do some Googling.

Tuesday morning, I marched up the stairs to my office, organizing my thoughts. Stephanie's paper had been patched together from several online essay sites, and now I had to deal not only with her but also with the student judicial committee. She had also used paragraphs from different pieces of literary criticism, one of which I'd recently happened to read, which is why I recognized it. I'd emailed her to arrange a meeting first thing this morning.

I stopped in the main office to get the necessary paperwork and found a smiling middle-aged woman with cat's eye glasses efficiently distributing flyers into department mailboxes.

"Hi," I said. "I'm Lila Maclean. American Lit."

"So happy to meet you," she said. "I'm Glynnis Klein, the new executive assistant. Just started this week." We'd had a parade of temps since the woman who had previously held her position had left. I'd heard the department had hired a permanent replacement, but this was the first time I'd met her.

"Welcome to Stonedale," I said. "How's it going so far? Everyone treating you well, I hope?"

"Absolutely," she said, with what could only be described as a wiggle of delight. She smoothed the front of the tailored cardigan she wore with a straight skirt, oxfords, and a huge flower brooch made of different colored gems. The ensemble had a certain retro pizzazz. "I adore Judith—she took me out to breakfast this morning and gave me the rundown on the faculty members. I feel as though I already know you all."

"Where were you before this?"

"I worked in the dean's office at the University of Nebraska for twelve years, but my husband was hired to teach in the Criminal Justice department here, so I came with him." She laughed and smoothed the side of her glossy brown hair, which was pulled back into a twist. "Obviously."

"Welcome," I said. "We're glad to have you with us."

Glynnis thanked me warmly and asked if she could be any help today. I explained that I was looking for plagiarism forms and she whirled around, opened a file cabinet, and plucked one out instantly.

At my look of surprise, she said, "I spent the better part of yesterday getting up to speed on where everything was."

I planned right then and there to try and make her feel as welcome as possible. I could already tell how lucky we were to have her.

"I'm not going to get *any* points for this?" Stephanie was tilting forward in the chair next to my desk, staring at me incredulously.

"Right."

"But I wrote it."

"Well, it appears to have complete sections from other sources, which renders the whole thing problematic."

"I did research," she said. "I thought that's what we're supposed to do."

"But research requires you to acknowledge your sources."

She sputtered. "But isn't *The Wasteland* about stealing other people's things to make something new? So," she said, thrusting out her chin, "I was doing that too."

"That's not exactly how I'd describe *The Wasteland*, but I understand what you mean about creating something new. In the poem, T.S. Eliot is making a point about a broken literary tradition after World War I and having to grasp at any fragments left in order not to be completely lost. It is transformative in its use of existing texts. And poets do refer to each other's work, as you know, which is called allusion and is part of the art."

She nodded, looking smug. "Exactly."

"But in the art of the essay, although we may also certainly quote other writers, it's a different genre, with different rules. We have a required system in place for documenting authors. For giving credit where credit is due. We need citations and a works cited list. And I don't see that here at all in your paper."

She looked somewhat less smug.

"How about we go over the rules for proper documentation," I suggested, picking up the MLA handbook and beginning to open it.

"I already know how to do it," she snapped.

"So you just chose not to do it this time?" I asked, as gently as I could.

That earned me a glare. "I forgot."

"Okay. Well, please try to remember in the future." I smiled, though I didn't feel like it, and set the handbook back on my desk.

"Can't I just add the citations now?"

"I'm sorry, but it's too late on this assignment."

After explaining to Stephanie she would be hearing from the

student judicial committee, I handed back her essay. Glynnis had made a copy of it for me to go with the required paperwork, which was on its way to Randsworth via campus mail.

Stephanie grabbed her backpack and left in a huff.

This was probably my least favorite part of the job so far.

Chapter 8

Thursday before the panel was clear and bright: Colorado putting on its best weather for our guests seemed like a positive sign. I allowed a glimmer of hope to penetrate the cloud of anxiety that had surrounded me since I'd heard Damon Von Tussel would be coming to Stonedale. I'd hoped I wouldn't be called upon to engage with him one on one, but the chancellor had made it clear that all members of the planning committee would be attending a small dinner at Judith and Spencer's tonight in Damon's honor, so even if he didn't attend the panel I was facilitating, I would have to be in a small space with the man eventually. Oh well. My mother had forgiven him, so there was nothing between us which needed negotiating. I could simply be professional.

Francisco had asked me to come early to the five o'clock panel. I passed the administration building, Randsworth Hall, which dominated the north side of campus. The gargoyles perched on the edge of the upper levels appealed to my Gothic sensibilities. Though many found their existence baffling and inexplicable, my humble opinion was that they added a certain whimsical charm to the campus. The designer had been a close friend of the university founder, Jeremiah Randsworth, and had been given carte blanche. He was also responsible for the pair of stone gryphons positioned at Stonedale's main gates as well as the underground passageways linking many of the buildings together—though not everyone knew about those.

When I'd almost reached Brynson Hall, which housed the

auditorium where the panel would take place, I saw Francisco on the sidewalk speaking to our colleague Tad Ruthersford, who taught early British literature. Both held tall coffee cups—it was a miracle Francisco wasn't spilling his all over, the way he was waving it around. As I drew closer, he caught my eye and frantically beckoned me over.

"Hi guys," I said.

Tad turned his blond head in my direction. "Milady," he said, toasting me with his paper cup. I smiled at him, glad to see my neighbor—we'd not had much of a chance to talk yet this semester because of opposing schedules.

"Are you ready to moderate the panel, Lila?" Francisco asked.

"Yes," I said. I had spent the two days prior reviewing the biographies and abstracts Francisco had given me for the necessary introductions and skimming the published articles of the panelists which were, not surprisingly, heavy on theory. I'd taken some time to prepare questions to which I could refer if discussion lagged during the question-and-answer session too. I was as ready as I was ever going to be.

"Good," Francisco said, "thanks." He looked exhausted. He probably hadn't been sleeping well—perfecting a presentation could be painstaking work. Especially when there was a chance the subject of your work might pop in and listen to what you're saying about them.

"Is everything okay?" I asked.

"Well, Damon's here," he said glumly.

"Isn't that good?"

"He hasn't been able to drive him around yet," Tad informed me, taking a sip of his coffee.

"Why not?"

Francisco tore off his black glasses and rubbed his eyes as he explained, "Jasper Haines is doing it. He rented a car."

I recognized the name. "Jasper's one of the panelists, right? The graduate student?" The others were assistant professors.

"Yes," said Francisco. "Just about to defend his dissertation.

He texted me this morning and said my services would not be needed."

"That's weird," I said, taken aback. "Did he say it like that?"

"Yes, but it's not weird at all if you know Jasper," Francisco said bitterly.

Francisco's chance to have the famous author to himself had been eliminated—and he'd been curtly dismissed to boot. That had to sting.

"Sorry, mate," said Tad. "I know you were looking forward to it."

Francisco started, embarrassed to be caught in a vulnerable moment. "Nothing to be sorry about. I'm relieved. Now I can just focus on my own presentation." No one believed him but we smiled at him supportively. "I'll see Damon at the dinner tonight anyway, so I'll just talk to him then."

Tad lightly clapped him on the back. "Good man. Roll with the punches."

"How well do you know Jasper?" I asked.

"Just from the Von Tussel Society," said Francisco, taking a sip of his coffee.

"Are you friends?" I persisted.

"No. More like acquaintances. We're both officers of the society."

"You're the president, right?" Tad interjected.

"Yes. He's the historian," Francisco said.

"Do you know if Damon will be at the presentation?"

Francisco looked even more weary, which I didn't think was possible until that moment. "I have no idea. Can't even worry about it. I'm more concerned right now about that email warning us not to let Damon read. You know the one I mean, Lila?"

"I do. Spencer also received one, and he said he would inform the proper authorities. Did he talk to you about it?"

"Yes. Everyone on the committee was sent the same email, apparently," Francisco said, taking a few steps away to chuck his coffee cup into a bin nearby. "Crazy."

Tad put his hand up, palm out, as if stopping traffic. "What are you talking about?"

We provided the details, and he shook his head. "And no reason was given for the emailer's belief that Damon shouldn't read?"

"No." A thought struck, unnerving me further. "Do you guys think it's related to the library incident? That would mean the person who emailed is already on campus, and it would ratchet up the danger level quite a bit."

Francisco slid a hand over his mouth and rubbed his chin. "I prefer to think it's just a crank. And I hope the manuscript is found. It's an incredible loss to literary history otherwise."

"Unbearable," Tad agreed.

Francisco sighed. "In any case, there's a panel to run. Let's go inside...I need to make sure everything is set up correctly."

We followed him into Brynson and down the short hallway to the double doors leading into the auditorium. I noticed he paused for a long moment to lean against the door before opening it. Gathering his thoughts, I imagined. Or—the thought occurred to me—trying to stay upright.

"Are you sure you're feeling well?" I asked, somewhat concerned.

"Yes, Lila," he shot over his shoulder. "I'm perfectly fine." He clomped down the sloped floor toward the front of the auditorium, barking at the student at the lectern who had accidentally made the microphone screech during testing.

I followed, sending good thoughts in the unfortunate student's direction.

An hour later, the panelists were sitting at the table set up center stage, ready to begin. I'd met them and shown them to their places, and now they were talking amongst themselves, with Jasper Haines dominating the conversation, gesticulating wildly. It looked as though he were holding court. At the end of the table, Francisco faced away from the rest of the group. I wondered if it indicated an intentional snub and, if so, who was snubbing whom?

I was in the wings fighting a surprisingly strong case of nerves by doing some calming deep breaths. The panelists didn't even seem this nervous, I thought, annoyed at myself. Hearing the buzz of the crowd, I peeked around the red velvet curtains.

People were arriving—more students than I'd imagined, though I knew some professors had offered their classes extra credit points for attending. The auditorium was about half full so far.

Calista suddenly appeared next to me, resplendent in a deep purple dress and massive necklace of milky white stones set into a black intricate webbing; the effect was that of a shimmering spider web draped around her throat. "Just wanted to check in and see how you are. Ready?"

"No. Want to go instead?" I thrust the page of introductory notes I clutched in my damp palm toward her. "Feel free."

She laughed and gave me a quick hug. "Just act like you know what you're doing and roll with it."

That was pretty much my whole routine these days. Being a new professor had a steep learning curve, to say the least.

As she walked away, she turned back around to add, "You've got this, sweetie."

Peering out around the curtain edge, I watched more people arrive and take their seats. Most of my colleagues were there. I didn't see Damon though. Perhaps he didn't want to know what scholars said about his writing. Some writers—probably most of them, actually—were like that.

A soft touch on my arm caused me to shoot straight up in the air. I turned to find Spencer standing there, obviously amused. "A tad jumpy, are we?"

"Nerves," I said, grimacing.

"You'll be wonderful. Just wanted to check in, see how things are going."

"The panelists are ready to go."

"Fine, fine," he said. "Oh, and the chancellor has IT on the case."

I stared at him, confused. "IT?"

"Our tech people are trying to figure out who sent the email about Damon's reading."

Fingers crossed. It would be a huge relief to know who was responsible. It was starting to feel necessary to look over our shoulders every two seconds.

"It's probably just someone who takes pleasure in wreaking havoc from afar, anonymously."

"But if it's related to the manuscript disappearing, it might mean that the emailer is already at Stonedale."

His eyes widened, but he assumed a soothing tone nonetheless. "Excellent point, Lila. I'll share that theory with the appropriate parties. But try not to worry about it too much."

Easier said than done. And we both knew that part of his job in this situation was to try and keep faculty calm, no matter what was happening.

"Thanks, Spencer. Appreciate the update."

He smiled and wished me luck before he left. I returned to the curtain. A few minutes later, the house lights went down, signaling that it was time to begin. I moved out to the wooden lectern on the side of the stage and switched on the microphone, tapping it gently to be sure it was on.

"Welcome," I began. "Thank you for joining us today." My voice tended to shake when I read in public, as I'd discovered to my horror at my first conference presentation. I'd learned by experience that I had to refrain from looking up until I got my bearings. "This panel has been sponsored by the Damon Von Tussel Society, dedicated to studying the writing of the author. Stonedale University will welcome Mr. Von Tussel himself, author of the award-winning novel *The Medusa Variation*, here on Saturday night as part of the Twenty-First Century Arts and Culture Series." I went into information mode, and by the time I'd explained the particulars and thanked the generosity of the chancellor's office and the trustees and everyone else who needed to be thanked for making it all possible, my voice was steady. I lifted my eyes to the crowd.

"All of the presenters today will focus on Mr. Von Tussel's latest collection, *In Medias Res*. First, we have Dr. Alonzo Ferrara, of UCLA, who will be presenting a chapter from his book in progress, *Damon Von Tussel: Suprafabulist*." That sounded like an album title, I thought but did not say. Plunging ahead, I read the bio paragraph, which he—like the other panelists—had provided himself. The biography showcased his degrees and publication history, which included a book on Von Tussel's earlier novel. "Please join me in welcoming Dr. Ferrara." The audience clapped politely.

A painfully thin assistant professor in a dark brown suit walked to the lectern. He looked nervous, and I held my breath while he arranged his papers, but he surprised me by launching into an exuberant discussion of Damon's literary contributions by way of the "medion."

Francisco had made a good choice in scheduling Alonzo first, as he provided a surprisingly coherent and engaging lecture on what he called "a new form," giving examples from the collection as support. Any audience member who hadn't read Damon's book would at least have an idea of what the other panelists were talking about. He finished strong and was rewarded with the approval of the audience. As he passed my chair on the way back to his seat, he flashed me a wide smile.

After the applause died down, I introduced Dr. Gilles Valmont of Brown, a tidy assistant professor in a Ralph Lauren jacket; he, too, had published one book on Von Tussel and was working on a second. Between multiple readjustments of his horn-rimmed glasses, he explained his reading of the multiple characters in the collection as fragments of one divided psyche which had been splintered by the oppressive forces of postmodernity, especially capitalism. The audience applauded at the conclusion of his thoughtful, if jargony, presentation.

Francisco walked up to the lectern after I'd read his biography aloud, which included an announcement of his own book in progress—*Spectral Liminality in the Work of Damon Von Tussel*. It sounded interesting, I reflected, as I returned to my chair, though you never knew with scholarly books if the content would be as interesting as the title.

Francisco paused dramatically, looking down at his notes before beginning. Just when the silence became uncomfortable, he smacked his hands together, the amplified sound reverberating around the auditorium. "*That*," he said, "is an aural representation of the ability of Damon Von Tussel to startle and to shock us. Over and over again, he says what has not been said, what should not be said, what is unsayable."

The man knew how to work a room.

"His characters are unable to escape their own longings, which take shape and function as unavoidable presences, hauntings." He spun off from there into an energetic argument of the "literary catapult" theory popularized by Damon himself as played out in the collection as a form of what Francisco called "the unavoidable assault into the deepest desires of the human mind." The audience stayed with him and gave him a deafening round of applause at the end. He bowed his head briefly, then returned to his seat.

"Our final reader is Jasper Haines," I said, relieved to be nearing the home stretch. "Mr. Haines comes to us from Columbia, where he is completing a dissertation entitled *Staring at Medusa: Damon Von Tussel and Infinite Play*."

"Which will be published next fall," Jasper said into the microphone when I'd stepped aside. "There are flyers in the front row, in case you want to pre-order," he added, running a hand over his spiky blond hair. There were a few chuckles from the crowd. He cleared his throat, wiped his brow, then began reading from the typed pages in front of him. "The omniplasticity of characters renders prototypical development obsolete—"

The audience gasped at the sickening thud made by the spotlight as it struck him on the head. He seemed to fold in half before sprawling on the ground, where he stopped moving. The room went completely silent for a moment, then all hell broke loose.

Chapter 9

The stage manager was protesting that he ran a tight ship around here, but no one was paying attention. The EMTs had taken Jasper to the hospital, the facilities crew had cleaned up the blood, and Campus Security had cleared the scene. Francisco, Calista, and I sat on the stage, as representatives of the department hosting this ill-fated event, waiting to be excused. We'd already filled out incident reports and given as much information as we could to whoever asked.

A pale Calista wondered aloud if Jasper had ever regained consciousness.

"No," I said. "He was still out when they put him into the ambulance. Do you think he'll..." I faltered.

"Live? You never know with head injuries," said Francisco. "And that light hit him so hard."

"Just a few moments earlier, both of you were standing in the exact same spot as Jasper," said Calista. "Are you freaked out?"

"I am," I said. "Not going to lie."

Francisco didn't respond.

I tried to change the subject. "Do you think Damon's reading will still take place?"

He turned slowly to me, as if struggling to process what I had just asked. He gave his head a shake. "Why wouldn't it?"

"Well..." I extended my arm and gestured to the nearly empty auditorium.

"It was an accident, Lila. I don't think it affects anything," said Francisco.

"What do you mean?"

"Let me put it this way: do you think Chancellor Wellington is going to eat the cost of the very expensive event because a visiting student got an owie?"

"It's more than an 'owie,' Francisco," I said, surprised.

"Okay, okay. Sorry." He put his hands up in surrender.

We fell quiet. The accident had probably shaken him more than he wanted to admit. I wasn't feeling particularly steady myself.

A plump man in a black Campus Security uniform eventually approached us. A small rectangular nametag on his chest read "Officer Stanley."

"You folks can leave now," he said gruffly.

"Sure we can't help with anything?" Calista said as she scooted off the edge of the stage.

"Nope."

"Thanks for coming so quickly," I said.

"Well, we weren't too far away when we got the call from dispatch." He smoothed his bristly brown mustache without any visible reduction in volume. It poked out in all directions from his upper lip.

We bid him goodbye and retired to the small room backstage where our coats and bags were piled. As we donned them, Francisco's cell phone rang. He scrabbled in his pocket for a moment, then pressed the screen and put the phone to his ear.

"What? I don't—"

He darted an angry glance at me. Uh oh.

"No, I'll find out and call you back." He clicked off without saying goodbye.

"What happened?" Calista and I said in unison.

"Damon didn't show up at Judith's," Francisco said. "He was supposed to be there for dinner at six o'clock, but now it's"—he consulted his heavy black watch—"almost seven."

"Seriously?" asked Calista.

Francisco's voice rose. "First Jasper, now this? What's going on?"

Calista patted his back and he shook her off while he glared at me. "Simone said you were in charge of arranging a student to escort him, Lila. Did you forget?"

Simone. Of course.

"No, Simone said *she* would do it."

"She just told me you were in charge."

"No, *she* was." I sounded like a child denying responsibility. "You know what? We could go get him. He's staying at the Mountain Inn. It's only a few blocks away."

Francisco perked up. "I'll drive."

"Can you call him and tell him we'll pick him up right now?" I knew Francisco had wrangled Damon's number from Spencer somehow and was the only one of us who even had it. Part of it was Damon's insistence on secrecy—of course his phone number was unlisted—but I suspected the other part was Francisco not wanting to share his famous author contact with the rest of us. Fine by me. I had no desire to call Damon Von Tussel.

Francisco dialed and listened intently for a few minutes, then jabbed the screen. "He's not answering."

"Then let's go over there and find him." I turned to Calista. "Could you please call Judith and let her know what's going on? Thanks so much—and we'll meet you there?" She nodded and rushed out without another word.

As we walked toward Francisco's Jeep Cherokee, I had a eureka moment and pulled out my own phone. If anyone could get ahold of Damon, it was my mother. She answered right away.

"Darling, how did the panel go? I've been on pins and—"

I cut her off while hoisting myself up and into the Jeep. "Mom, sorry but I need your help. We can't find Damon—"

"Again?"

"I mean, he's here in town, but he's not where he's supposed to be at the moment. We're trying to deliver him to a dinner in his honor. Could you please call him?"

"I'll try. What should I say?"

"If he's at the hotel, tell him to stay put. Francisco and I—"

"Ooh, Francisco? What a dashing name. He sounds interesting."

"He's a colleague, Mom. Please tell Damon to stay at the Mountain Inn and we'll pick him up. If he's somewhere else, call me back and let me know where to go."

"I'll get back to you in a minute either way." She hung up.

I looked over at Francisco, who was checking his phone while the Jeep warmed up.

"I'll send Damon a text too." He tapped quickly, then dropped his phone into the beverage holder and backed out of the parking spot.

We made it to the Mountain Inn in three minutes. Francisco pulled up to the front door and I ran inside to the front desk, where a bored-looking woman in a blue polyester uniform lifted her overly plucked eyebrows at my haste.

"Help you?" she asked.

"I'm looking for Damon Von Tussel," I said.

Her fingers didn't exactly fly across the keyboard of the computer in front of her, but she was pressing keys. I tried to be patient, studying the taupe walls, which were finished in a fake stone texture. Finally, she looked up. "Extension 6642. You can call up to his room right there," she said, pointing across the lobby to a phone on a small oval table next to a sofa printed with a vaguely southwestern design in brown and mauve.

As I walked toward the chipped end table, my cell rang. I glanced at the screen. It was my mother. "Hello?"

"He'll be waiting for you in the lobby," she said.

I looked around, confused. "I'm in the lobby."

"We just finished talking. He'll be there in a sec."

"Mom, you're the best. Thank you so much. Talk later?"

"I know you have to go. Good luck, darling. Call me tomorrow," she said.

I promised to do so, and we hung up. The elevator dinged

around the corner, and I took a few steps in that direction. Anxiety welled up in my stomach, but I reminded myself I had no choice but to speak to him. I straightened my shoulders. Then Damon appeared dressed in a well-cut navy suit and a paisley tie. The mahogany cane with the gleaming silver tip was a new affectation. It was clearly unnecessary: he charged down the hallway toward me like a bull. I braced myself for our conversation.

The odor of whiskey on his breath reached me before he did. "Lila," he said in his gravelly voice.

"Hello, Damon. I'm here to take you to the dinner. I'm afraid we had a mix-up with the student who was to escort you over there—I'm sorry."

He shrugged philosophically. "S'allright. I knew someone would come eventually."

The elevator dinged again and a woman with bronze streaks in her long brunette hair joined us. She wore a red tunic-length sweater over a long black skirt. Very little makeup—just some mascara and lip gloss—and gorgeous. I'd guess about twenty-five years old. How had he hooked up with someone so soon, especially since no one has made arrangements for students to help him get around campus?

"Do you have my coat?" she asked.

He smiled fondly at her as he tapped a leather jacket across his lower arm. I'd been so focused on the cane on the other side that I hadn't even noticed it was there.

She slipped the jacket on, then turned to me. "Who's this, then?"

I put out my hand. "I'm Lila Maclean."

"Violet's daughter?" She squeezed my hand painfully.

"Yes," I said, surprised. "You know my mother?"

"Of course." She pointed to herself. "I'm Mina." She seemed to expect me to know who she was. At my blank look, she added, "Damon's daughter."

"Oh, I didn't know you were coming out to Colorado." I tried to phrase it so she wouldn't know I had no idea Damon even *had* a daughter. I didn't remember my mother ever mentioning her. "Nice to meet you."

"And you," she said warmly. "I'm surprised we never ran into each other in New York."

"I didn't go out much in recent years because I was working on my dissertation."

She asked some questions about my project, then I turned the conversation back to her.

"Have you lived in the city your whole life?"

"Oh. I grew up there, then I was off to boarding school, then college. Came back to New York two years ago—" she began.

Damon interrupted. "We've just been—" He made a circling motion with his hand while he searched for the word.

"Reunited," Mina offered. Her smile was wide over extremely white teeth, and her whole face lit up.

"Glad you decided to return," said Damon, clumsily knocking her with his shoulder.

"Aw, me too," she said to her father. She stepped back and hugged Damon fiercely, almost knocking him over.

"That's...great," I said.

I couldn't help reflecting on the fact that my mother had never told me who my own father was. But I had chosen to respect her wishes and not push for more information. Not that I never wondered about him. Perhaps I should utilize some of my scholarly skills and do some tracking of my own. I'd been tempted before, but I didn't want to hurt my mother's feelings. Still, didn't I have a right to know? I could feel myself spiraling down familiar, complicated territory. I resolutely shoved the line of thought away and smiled at them both.

"Are you coming to dinner, Mina?"

"They know you're bringing me, right?" She turned to Damon.

He raised and lowered his shoulders quickly. "I don't know anything about anything."

Mina's face fell.

"I'm sure it will be fine," I said, planning to text Judith on the way over in case she didn't know already. "And will your mother be joining us too?"

Mina froze, a shadow crossing her face. "No."

"Her mother is Minerva," Damon said quietly. "The supermodel."

Oh no. Minerva was a friend of my mother's. It had been widely publicized that she'd died of a drug overdose a number of years ago.

"I'm so sorry," I said.

Mina nodded. I apologized again.

Damon looked back and forth between us. "Shall we go? I'm thirsty."

Judith Westerly met us in the foyer of the spacious home she shared with Spencer. As she opened her arms to greet us, the sleeves of her long golden gown fluttered gracefully. "Welcome!"

"Sorry we're late," I said, which she waved away, then patted the back of her silver chignon.

"Not a problem at all. We happily extended our cocktail hour until the guest of honor could arrive." She floated up to Damon and extended her hand. "Dear Mr. Von Tussel, we are so grateful you're here. I'm looking forward to your reading tremendously."

As he took the hand of his slim host, he looked genuinely charmed. Judith had that effect on people—her profuse kindness tended to wrap itself around you like the coziest of blankets. "Come right this way," Judith said. "I've just sent everyone into the dining room."

Everyone followed her obediently, including Damon, whose cane tapped loudly on the marble floors. I realized that I'd forgotten to text Judith about Mina, and I needed to remedy the situation. I wasn't even sure Judith had seen Mina at the back of the group.

"Why don't you wait here, and I'll grab Judith so you two can meet?" I asked Mina.

She hesitated.

"She's very nice," I assured her.

"Thank you," she said quietly.

I hurried over to Judith and explained the situation. She apologized for not introducing herself to Mina and told me to go on ahead. As she turned to go back to the main entrance, she whispered to one of the servers walking nearby—no doubt graciously arranging for a chair to be whisked into place for her party crasher.

I went through the doorway into which Judith had led Damon, to the left. I followed the sound of voices, moving quickly past the sofa in the great room where I'd sat, trembling, as Detective Archer had taken my statement last fall. No need to relive that. We finally reached the dining room near the back of the house and entered. My colleagues were chatting, drinks in hand, as they approached the beautifully set long table. The crystal shone and the silver gleamed in the warm yellow light of the chandelier. There were four small white bouquets brightening the center of the large table—low enough for all guests at the table to converse; Judith paid attention to things like that.

After a moment, Judith returned and took her place at the far end of the table, wagging her hands to indicate we should all take our seats. Spencer sat at the end of the table opposite her. Damon—who had somehow managed to score himself a glass of whiskey in the nanosecond since we'd arrived—already slumped with his elbows on the table beside Judith, and Mina took the chair next to him. I settled beside her, smiling at Nate who had obtained the seat next to me. Norton took the last seat on our side. I saw Chancellor Wellington whispering to Spencer before claiming the seat next to him across the table. He was followed in rapid succession by Simone, Dean Okoye, Calista, and Francisco. Tolliver was a no-show, as usual.

Simone and I were going to have a talk later about her sabotage, that's for sure. She knew it, too, avoiding eye contact with me, though she twinkled at Nate across the table.

Two young men in white shirts and black pants circled the

table, placing bone china plates with filet mignon, new potatoes, and asparagus spears before us. Silence fell over the table, and we all picked up our forks and began to eat the delicious food.

Damon smacked his lips and gave his beard a stroke. "First-rate eats," he rumbled.

A chorus of appreciation followed the guest of honor's lead.

"Thank you for the kind words," said Judith. "Please let me know if you need anything at all."

"Good thing someone finally remembered to pick us up or we'd have missed this meal," Damon said to Mina, unleashing a phlegmy staccato laugh.

Mina's lips curved up. She was clearly ignoring her father's boorish behavior.

The servers reappeared with carafes of red wine and circled the table, refilling glasses. I admired the professional twirl at the end they performed and wondered how long it had taken to master the maneuver.

"Any news on Jasper?" Simone inquired of Francisco.

"Jasper Haines?" Damon froze, the next bite of filet mignon halfway to his mouth.

We hadn't talked about the panel in the car, as focused as we were on speeding across town to the gathering. Instead, I'd let Francisco chat with Damon and Mina, knowing he'd been deprived of the opportunity before by the machinations of his rival. I'd tuned out after the first tidal wave of admiration.

"What happened?" Damon barked, letting the hand with the fork fall on the table.

"Oh, I thought you knew..." Simone blanched slightly. Mina and Damon stared at her with puzzled expressions.

"There was an accident during the panel," Francisco said. "While Jasper was presenting his paper, a stage light fell on him."

Mina gasped, and her hands flew up to cover her mouth. Damon didn't move, but he let out a hard breath of air, as if he'd been punched in the stomach.

"Is he okay?" he said urgently.

It was silent for a long moment, then everyone spoke at once.

"He had just begun speaking—" said Norton.

"He's still alive—" said Nate.

"The light just came crashing down—" said Simone.

"He probably has a severe—" said Dean Okoye.

"Shall I call the hospital right now—" said Judith.

"A most unfortunate incident—" said Spencer.

Damon looked from speaker to speaker, trying to make sense of the flood of words.

Finally, Francisco spoke loudly enough to quell the din. "They took him to Stonedale Hospital. I was going to stop by on the way home and check on him." That surprised me, given his feelings about Jasper. But perhaps Francisco was more bark than bite. "If anyone would like to join me, I'd be glad for the company."

Damon looked down the long table at Judith. "We need to go check on him. Jasper is—" He faltered, locking eyes with Mina.

Mina was already standing, looking distressed. Were those tears in her eyes? "He's my fiancé," she said.

"I'll take you right now," said Francisco, putting his napkin on the table.

Suddenly, everyone seemed to be on their feet, milling around saying goodbyes.

I made my way to the other end of the table and apologized to Judith for leaving. "It was a lovely dinner, and I'm sorry I need to go, but Francisco's my ride."

She hugged me. "No worries, my dear. I do hope Mr. Haines is recovering. You'll keep me posted."

I agreed and followed Damon and Mina out to Francisco's car, not looking forward to what was sure to be a tense journey.

Chapter 10

Damon climbed into the passenger seat, and Mina followed me into the backseat of Francisco's Jeep Cherokee. As we drove down University Boulevard toward Stonedale Hospital, Damon asked us to walk him through what had happened. From my diagonal position in the back, I could see he was twisting the elegant cane next to his left leg anxiously.

Francisco gave him a quick look before answering. "Lila introduced Jasper, he walked up to the lectern, and then it happened."

"Had he started talking yet?" Damon asked.

"No," said Francisco.

"Wait," I interrupted. "He *had* begun speaking. I think he'd said a sentence or two, then the light knocked him on the ground."

"He was hit on the head? Was he bleeding?"

Francisco described the scene for him.

"Did he regain consciousness?" Mina asked, from the backseat.

"Not as far as we know," I said.

"What was his topic again?" Damon asked.

Francisco told him the title of the presentation and Damon nodded.

"Knew I should've gone," said Damon.

That seemed like a strange thing to say. Did he think if he'd been there, the accident wouldn't have happened?

"But Dad, you know it upsets you to hear people reading all kinds of things into your work," protested Mina. "That's why we didn't go."

He didn't say anything.

"You couldn't have prevented it," she continued, reaching around the seat in front of her to rub his arm, her voice soothing.

"And neither could you," he said to her.

"I'm the one who should have gone," she said sadly. "But I was trying to fight off this migraine before the dinner party."

She pressed her head with the top half of her hands and rocked back and forth.

No one spoke the rest of the way.

Francisco pulled up to the emergency room doors and Damon and Mina rushed inside. Francisco found a parking spot not too far away and turned off the engine.

He faced me. "Should we go inside?"

"We're giving them a ride home, right?"

"Yes."

"Then I say we go in."

After we'd gone through the sliding glass doors, we moved toward the large intake desk.

"If you're not family," I heard a stern-looking nurse say to Damon, "I can't tell you any more than that."

"I'm his fiancée," Mina said, stepping up to the desk and flashing a diamond ring. The nurse led her through two more double doors into the ER area.

The three of us sat in brightly colored plastic chairs in the waiting room. Damon made himself one coffee after another and Francisco checked his phone the whole time. I stared at the string of unfunny sitcoms with annoyingly loud laugh tracks on the television mounted high in the corner of the room. It didn't seem to set the right tone for an emergency room, but I didn't know how to change the channel.

After another half hour, Mina reappeared with Jasper in tow. He was moving slowly.

We stood to meet them.

"He has a concussion, but otherwise they think he's fine," Mina said.

"Got off easy," Damon said, looking Jasper up and down. "Good news."

"Glad you're okay," I said.

Jasper gave us a weak smile.

Mina took a firmer grip on his arm. "Let's get him back to the hotel."

We all exchanged looks of relief and walked silently to the car through the parking lot. The darkness was punctured here and there by street lamps casting an eerie orange glow on the concrete.

Once we were settled in the car again, it was an effort to fasten my seatbelt. I suddenly felt drained of all energy.

The ride was quiet for the most part, aside from an occasional groan from Jasper. He was slumped in the backseat next to Mina, resting his head on her shoulder. She murmured to him—sounded like words of encouragement, though I couldn't hear the specifics over the heat blasting out of the vents.

After we deposited the trio at the Mountain Inn, Francisco asked me where I lived.

"You can just drop me by campus," I said. "Or I can walk from here."

"No way," he said. "It's too late."

I gave him my address and he put the car in gear.

The tires on the pavement were almost lulling me to sleep, so I cracked my window about an inch. The fresh air revived me slightly.

"How well do you know Jasper?"

"Didn't you ask me the same question before the panel?" he snapped.

And here I thought we'd bonded tonight. Apparently not. A spark of anger shot through me.

"You don't have to rip my head off." I crossed my arms over my chest.

Francisco shook his head. "You're right."

I was?

When he stopped at the next red light, he turned toward me.

"It's not you. I cannot stand the guy, all right? As soon as he found out we were both writing a book about Damon, he made it a contest. He kept emailing me to check in, he said, but it was really to brag about how much he'd written. He raced me to the finish line, and—" He let out a deep breath. "He won. His book is coming out soon, and I'm still in the submission process."

"But yours will be great," I said. Listening to him tonight had been fascinating. "And it doesn't matter who's first," I added, in an attempt to comfort him.

"Except that it does. Which you know, Lila."

"But you're not writing on exactly the same topic, are you?"

"He's writing about *The Medusa Variation* too, but we both discuss *In Medias Res.*"

"Francisco, according to the introductions tonight, every one of the panelists has a book coming out on Von Tussel's most recent collection."

He sighed again. "I know. But Jasper is the only one who taunted me the whole way through. I finally had to block him from sending me emails because he was really getting inside my head."

"He sounds like a stalker."

"He kind of was." Francisco gripped the steering wheel tightly. "Plus, he kept hinting he knew something I didn't, that his book would somehow invalidate my book. Mine would already be out there, too late for me to recall, and it would be wrong. I can't have that. I obviously need the book to be correct in order to be taken seriously for tenure."

"Had you ever shown him a draft?"

"No, but we'd presented at a bunch of the same conferences on the same panels. That's how we met."

"You've heard his papers?"

"Yes."

"And was there anything in them which was especially groundbreaking?"

"Not at all."

"What do you think he meant?"

"I've spent the past months racking my brain over that very question. I can hardly sleep anymore."

Curiouser and curiouser.

Spencer had somewhat embarrassedly asked all the faculty members to find a way to insert a Von Tussel text or two into our respective class activities. He thought it might engage the students and, of course, sell more tickets. I had a copy of *The Medusa Variation* from grad school, and my mother had sent along *In Medias Res* when it was published, though I had never read the latter. Time to remedy that. Since I didn't own any wine glasses, I poured myself a generous tumbler of cabernet and added a handful of ice cubes—blasphemous behavior, according to oenophile friends of my mother—and sank on the sofa. After taking a sip, I flipped the book open to a random section.

The Writer
I pass the group clustered like so many baboons on the steps of the coffeehouse, noting their carefully arranged signs of intellectualism, the startlingly black glasses against the pale poet's skin, the regimented black turtleneck framing carefully unkempt hair, cultivated bohemian markers. They are poseurs. They are fragile. With one wave of my hand I could disperse them, dandelion puffs scattered over the pavement. But I have no time for such easy revenge.

The hellhole is packed today. I cast a glance about the pretentious snots dotting the tables. A woman in a crushed red velvet dress laughs, exposing a neck made of alabaster. A potential gothic heroine right in the middle of my scenario. How fitting. Welcome to my castle.

A boy stalks up to the podium and fumbles into the microphone, which squeaks when he touches it. I am pleased with his ineptitude. He reddens but clears his throat authoritatively. "Hello," he says, "and welcome to Café Idiosyncratique's weekly poetry celebration." The room silences slowly as audience members drag their heads toward the stage. The boy blathers on about tipping servers appropriately, then introduces the first reader. He snaps his fingers, which prompts a similar action from the audience, like sheep with muted castanets.

I stifle a laugh. The efforts are too painful to watch. I won't make a move yet, though, as it is too early for what I have in mind.

Well, although I disliked the tone, I had to admit he had satirized something of the vibe that could permeate a performative sphere. I wasn't sure it qualified as a fully developed short story or even flash fiction, though. Turning the page, I began reading the next piece.

The Professor

He is reading an article, just one in a giant tower of pages collected in another round of painstaking research. The title promises a psychoanalytic take on a book he is "working on"— such a bland phrase to summarize the years of dogged, careful effort, the excruciatingly quiet hours spent in a sort of anxious haze of synthesis, knowing he had things to say but not how they fit together, aware that with every passing day the likelihood of his being "scooped," to use the vulgar cliché, increased exponentially. He had cocooned himself in his topic, it was his small "area of expertise," as the saying goes. Long sessions before the glowing keyboard or in the dusty stacks holding the triumphant evidence of others' ability to complete such projects had honed his sense of endeavor: he thought himself a warrior involved in meaningful pursuits, despite (or perhaps because of) receiving no monetary gain for the painful, noble inquiry. Pale skin, spongy flesh, and clawed hands signify their own kind of honor.

When he begins to process what he's reading, he can hear his heartbeat echoing loudly in his ears. It can't be...but it is. There before him in ravaging splendor is the bulk of his insight: the article discusses every point he's labored to birth in practically the same order and with exactly the same evidence but, and here's the worst part, in language more precise, more lively, more fluid, and more engaging than anything he could imagine mustering, even on his best day. He glimpses the implications all at once: the research guaranteed to solidify his tenure bid demolished; the probable end of his marriage, as his wife could hardly handle his terse, ghostly presence as it was; the smug satisfaction of his colleagues who had already begun making pointed comments at departmental gatherings, served up with the fancy cheeses and cheap wines. He knows the absolute necessity of finding a new angle as quickly as possible. How could one devote one's life to something so completely and then, in the name of all that is sweetness and light, have this happen?

He scans the article again, fighting to control the shriek welling up from within. Then slowly, deliberately, aims his shaking hands toward the keyboard.

Damon had certainly captured the potential angst of academic life. With this one, more than the previous selection, I felt simultaneously eager to know what happened next and annoyed that I never would. Maybe there was something to this experiment—though Damon would never label it an experiment. He would—in fact he had—describe "the medion" as "an intentional literary catapult," which would force readers into imagining the endings themselves, so no reader would experience the same text exactly the same way. I'd rolled my eyes when I first read snippets of much longer pontifications in interviews, but I had to admit it was effective in exposing our readerly expectations about fiction.

These might actually work as comparisons in my Modernism class, where we were studying authors who overtly experimented. And helpfully wrote lots of manifestos explaining why.

*   *   *

The next morning was almost aggressively sunny and much warmer. I emailed my classes, reminding them of the workshop with Damon. It was a unique opportunity, open only to students and English faculty. I hoped they would take advantage of it, especially those with literary aspirations, though I know some students might prefer to hit the slopes instead. It was Friday, after all.

I didn't have to go to campus until later, so I signed out of the Stonedale website and pulled up my Isabella Dare book proposal to do one last proofreading pass.

Francisco's situation flashed through my head as I waited for the document to open. The success of his book would matter to Francisco's tenure bid—not that it had to be a bestseller, but it certainly needed to be respectable. The more I thought about Jasper's behavior, the worse I felt for Francisco. Writing a book was incredibly hard work—to have finally completed one only to be told your ideas were most likely incorrect would be unbearable. More to the point, why would Jasper do it? I knew many people in academia were highly competitive, but this bordered on downright bullying.

Several hours later, I'd finished proofing the proposal and sample chapters. I pulled up the website of my first-choice university press; thank goodness you could do these things online nowadays. I'd made a list of my top ten over break and was planning to work my way through it if necessary. Carefully, I filled out the required information and attached the necessary documents. I paused at end of the form, almost talking myself out of it, then steeled my resolve—I had to start sometime, right?—and clicked "Submit."

A flash of joy, followed by a wave of terror.

So that's what submitting a book felt like.

I glanced at the clock and realized that I needed to hurry if I wanted to make the workshop. After a quick shower and an even quicker lunch, I shoved a thick black wrap into my bag—you never knew in Colorado when you might need another layer—and walked over to campus for the workshop, which began at four. After a few blocks, I realized I had more energy than I'd felt in a long time. Submitting the proposal had rejuvenated me somehow. Maybe it was just that instead of worrying about what I had to do in the future, I'd finally taken some action. Regardless of what happened, I could at least know I'd tried.

I strode past Pennington Library and recognized Mina walking toward me, accompanied by Tally Bendel. I hadn't realized Damon's agent was here in Stonedale.

I waved, and we all quickened our steps to meet each other in the middle.

Tally was clad in a fringy leather coat and pants, with extremely high stilettos and a bulky bag slung over one shoulder. She was typing with her thumbs on her phone as she walked, and she barely looked up to acknowledge my presence. Mina wore another tunic and long skirt today—both were in a becoming shade of bronze that matched the streaks in her hair. Her wrists were covered in at least two dozen thin gold bangles which audibly jingled until she stopped just in front of me.

"Lila. So glad I ran into you. Could you please point us in the direction of Crandall Hall?"

I pointed across the green. "I'm heading there now for the workshop. Shall we go together?"

She smiled gratefully and we began walking. When I asked where Damon was, Mina informed me that he wasn't coming.

Chapter 11

"I'm going to lead the workshop instead," Mina said. "My father isn't feeling well."

"I'm sorry to hear that. Is it serious?"

"He'll bounce back before his reading." Tally dropped the arm holding her phone to her side, fringe flying. I had the feeling her phone was never much farther away from her than that. "You understand, doll."

I didn't, but I should have expected that Damon wouldn't show up after hearing rumors about how he treated his teaching jobs. "Have you let Spencer know about the change of plans?"

Tally assumed a patient look beneath her thick layers of makeup. "Of course. And Mina here is fabulous, just terrific." She squeezed Mina's arm. "You're lucky she's available."

"Lila, I know it isn't ideal," Mina said apologetically. "But I'll try to give an insider portrait of my father, and hopefully the audience will enjoy it."

"Great," I said, my mind skittering off to imagine what the chancellor would have to say about this. He'd probably find a way to blame me for this too. "Well, follow me."

I addressed Tally as we walked. "Nice to see you again. I didn't know you were in town. Do you go to all of Damon's events?"

"Heck no," she said, with a short, loud bray. "I was in Aspen for a ski vacation. A long overdue one at that—my clients are marvelous, but they wear me out. You know what I mean." She clutched Mina with her red talons. "Anyway, his publisher called and demanded I make sure the Colorado events went off without a hitch."

"But the Denver reading—"

"I know, doll. It was a hot mess." She shrugged. "He's a handful. But I got him back here for you, didn't I?"

I refrained from pointing out that it was my mother, as far as I knew, who had convinced Damon to honor his contract. Plus the doubled fee.

"Leave it to me. Tally's got your back. He'll show up this week."

She seemed to have forgotten that the workshop we were heading toward at this very instant was supposed to involve Damon showing up.

"Hello, everyone," Mina said to the classroom of attendees. The room was completely full—every chair was occupied and people leaned against all conceivable real estate along the back and side walls. The administration would certainly be pleased by the turnout. "I'm sorry to have to announce my father won't be here today. He has fallen ill." She paused while the sounds of surprise and displeasure dissipated. "But he has sent me as a replacement, and I hope I'll be able to make the workshop worth your while. I do teach creative writing, so I will share some techniques with you, but more importantly for this gathering, I will tell you about my father's own writing process."

I had to give her credit for remaining calm in front of an obviously disgruntled audience. She smiled disarmingly, and the tension subsided slightly.

"Obviously, Damon Von Tussel is a genius," she said, going into a description of the book which had garnered him so many accolades. "But after *The Medusa Variation*, he couldn't finish a story for several decades."

The sun through the window to her left reflected off of her bronze clothes and highlights, making her glow. You could feel the attention in the room rising as she continued to speak. She was like some kind of fairy tale creature, spinning her web of words around us. I noticed a number of my Modernism students sitting in the front few rows. They were listening intently, and Keandra was busily taking notes.

"He wrote every day. It was just that after a certain amount of time, he would lose interest. His one constant thought was this: 'If it's boring me, it will bore everyone else too.' Those of you who write are familiar with such fear—right?" She raised an eyebrow and heads around the room began to nod.

"So," she said, warming to her topic, "he told himself he would write one story a month until one of them caught fire." She smiled. "Metaphorically, of course. Every month, he would start a new story. And by the end of the month, he would have abandoned it. Eventually, he tried to begin at the end of the story instead, thinking he could write his way back toward the initial scene somehow. But that didn't work either. This went on for years. He wrote and wrote and wrote, without finishing anything."

She paused and looked slowly around the room. "A lesser author might have quit. He wasn't publishing anything—why bother? But my father is nothing if not determined. Eventually, it came to him." She held up a fist, then she twisted her wrist upright and unfolded her fingers slowly, like a flower blooming. The gold bangles jingled emphatically and her voice grew louder. "If the middle part was what he loved best, then why not just write the middle? That's where all the action is, anyway. And *In Medias Res* was born."

The audience broke out into applause. She bowed her head gracefully and walked over to the whiteboard. Uncapping the black pen, she wrote FIND THE HEART OF YOUR STORY.

"Now, let's do some writing."

After the audience members were guided through several creative exercises by Mina, the workshop ended.

Nate slid into the seat next to me.

"Hey, you. What do you think?"

"She's a very talented teacher," I said. "Engaging. I think my students really enjoyed it."

"Agreed." He patted his legs in a sort of drum roll. His jeans had a hole in the knee, which was endearing somehow. "Did you?"

"It was interesting," I said. "I didn't know Damon had trouble producing anything. I thought he was just coasting on the success of the first book, I guess."

"I'd never heard that before...but I dig hearing how authors create. I wish I could have interviewed Nathaniel Hawthorne about it myself," he said, invoking his favorite author.

"Do you like Von Tussel's stories?"

He nodded. "They're cool. Do you?"

"Yes..." I paused.

"But..." he said, brows raised, encouraging me to finish my sentence.

I frowned, gathering my thoughts.

"Why Miz Lila, I do believe you have more to say."

"It's just...hmm. I guess I'm not clear on why Damon's work is so celebrated. A lot of contemporary fiction seems to do the same thing, leave out exposition and denouement. Heck, some of them even do far more fascinating things with form than he does."

"Ah," Nate said, stroking an imaginary beard. "Touché."

I rolled my eyes. "Seriously, though."

"Okay, you're right—half the stories I read these days don't seem to have beginnings or endings. Why *are* we all talking about this guy?"

We chuckled for a minute. Then Nate continued, "Come to think of it, he seems to have less of an arc than even some of the flash fictions I've read."

"That's true," I said slowly.

"Which makes it even more middle-centric."

"I see your point," I said.

Nate nodded thoughtfully. "But mostly I think it's because he wrapped up the collection in his 'literary catapult' theory. I'd love to write an article on how having both at once affects the reading experience, but Francisco's been working on his Von Tussel book for years. It's his thing. Don't want to cramp his style. But it's fascinating, anyway."

"That reminds me. I sent in my first proposal today."

"Good for you!" he said, giving my arm a small squeeze. "Where did you send it?"

We had fallen into a discussion of university presses and academic publishers when we were joined by drama professor Willa Hartwell, her chestnut curls piled on top of her head in a loose bun that was threatening to topple over.

"What are we debating?" she said in her melodious English accent, face alight with curiosity.

"Lila's book proposal," Nate said.

"Lovely. How is it going?" she asked, turning her full attention to me.

"Great, actually. I just sent it in today."

"You sent it in? Was it your study of Dare's work?"

"Yes," I said.

"Well, *that's* not going to be accepted," Willa said, zipping up her purple fleece vest.

"Oh," I said, temporarily at a loss for words.

"No harm done, I'm sure. You can always send it somewhere else." She nodded briskly, her coiffure sliding a few degrees to the east.

Nate looked as confused as I was. We exchanged glances, then he spoke up first. "What do you mean, Willa?"

Her eyes widened, as if stunned at our denseness. "Well, they aren't going to publish a critical study on an author no one has heard of."

She was probably right. I felt my body wilt.

"You'll need to send both proposals at once—or perhaps focus on getting the primary texts published in critical editions first, then submit your analytical study."

"They might go hand in hand, I think," I said slowly.

"Do let us have tea and talk about it at your earliest convenience," Willa implored. "I would love to help in whatever small way might be useful."

Anything other than bursting my tiny bubble of hope would have been nice. I knew her intentions were good, but: ow.

She sailed off, her proper carriage, as always, an inspiration, though I wasn't sure her hairdo would survive the next hour.

Nate patted my shoulder. "Don't listen to her. She's not the boss of you. And who knows? Maybe they'll take it anyway."

I shrugged. "It was only my first submission."

"There you go," he said. He surveyed the room, then jerked his head toward three of the panelists from last night—Gilles Valmont, Alonzo Ferrara, and Jasper Haines—clumped together in the back corner of the room. "Now, let's go say hello to Monsieur de Valmont and company."

That made me laugh.

"I dare you to call him Monsieur de Valmont to his face," I said, as we made our way along an empty row of chairs.

"Oh, ye of little faith," Nate retorted. "I'll recite a whole speech from *Dangerous Liaisons* if the price is right."

As we approached the circle of panelists in the corner, Mina flew past us and flung herself into Jasper's arms.

"You didn't have to come," she said as he hugged her.

"I wanted to. I'm fine," he said, kissing her. He looked fine too in a black leather jacket paired with jeans—just as hale and hearty as he had been when he strode up to the lectern.

"Hi everyone," Nate said. I waved at the general group.

"We were talking about the accident," said Alonzo, who looked less painfully thin today in a thick green fisherman sweater which brought to mind a turtle shell. He blinked several times in concert with the bobbing of his Adam's apple. There was more than a pinch of Ichabod Crane about him. "I'm still bothered."

"Me, too," said Gilles, his eyes slits behind his horn-rimmed glasses, which he readjusted carefully. His blue wool blazer had a crest on the pocket, but I couldn't see the design clearly. Even if I did, I probably wouldn't recognize what school it stood for. It could be Hogwarts for all I knew.

I would however be able to recognize the Stonedale University crest, which featured books and stars. Not too subtle, that. At one of our mentoring meetings, we'd received a sticker with the crest and the school motto, "Ever More," on it. We were instructed to "display it proudly." I'd thumbtacked mine to the bulletin board over my desk. Hope that counted.

"Don't stress about the accident," said Jasper. "Things happen."

"I hope you're feeling well," I said.

"Yup," said Jasper. He made a dismissive gesture with his free hand. The other was draped over Mina's shoulder. She gazed at him lovingly. "Luckily, Mina here kept an eye on me last night."

"And did I hear correctly that you two are engaged?" I smiled at them.

Mina blushed prettily. "Yes," she said, her generous mouth stretching into a dazzling smile. "He proposed at Christmas."

We all congratulated them.

"You didn't forget, right?" Mina said fondly. "With your concussion and all."

"I didn't forget," Jasper assured her, squeezing her against him. "Time to take it to the next level."

"Soon? Or..." one of the panelists said.

"We haven't had much time to plan, but we'd rather have a ceremony sooner rather than later." Mina looked into Jasper's eyes.

"Best wishes to you both," said Nate.

A cloud crossed Jasper's face.

"What?" the ever-attentive Mina asked gently.

"Campus Security called this morning. They told me the light didn't just fall. Someone messed with it. There's no way it could come loose by itself. It had to have been removed and thrown from the catwalk above the stage."

"What?" Mina shrieked.

"Don't worry," Jasper said to her. "I just wanted to tell Lila and

Nate to make sure someone has eyes on the catwalk before your father reads."

"Oh my God," wailed Mina. "Someone tried to hurt you on purpose? And may be going after my father? Why?"

Jasper shrugged helplessly.

"Do you have any enemies?" Nate asked.

"Not that I know of," Jasper said, looking uncomfortable.

"Does your father?" Nate addressed Mina.

"Not that I know of."

There was a long silence. Francisco's face popped into my mind, but he had been on the stage the whole time. He couldn't be in two places at once.

I turned to Mina. "We'll talk to the stage manager about securing the catwalk before your father reads."

They thanked me.

"So relieved you're better today, hon," Mina said, glowing up at Jasper. He pulled her close and nuzzled the top of her head.

It seemed time to make our exit.

Chapter 12

Outside, the air had turned cooler; I was grateful to have my wrap, which I threw around my shoulders. When we passed the edge of the building, I briefly contemplated the mauve and purple sunset over the mountains to the west. I didn't think I would ever get tired of the sight, and I was taking it in when I heard Francisco's voice.

"Lila and Nate—do you want to grab a bite?" he called.

I turned around to see him holding open the door of Crandall, through which Calista soon traipsed out.

Why not? All I had waiting at home was a can of soup. They caught up to us, and we headed toward The Peak House, a microbrewery a few blocks from campus. It was warm and inviting inside, crowded with people celebrating happy hour, but they were able to seat us right away in a large booth. We opened the menus to study them, then gave our orders to the server and settled in to wait.

"Hey, Dr. Maclean." I turned to find Keandra standing next to me, a glass of amber liquid in her hand. She set it down on the table. "Did you go to the workshop?"

"Yes," I said. "I was in the back. Did you like it?"

"Yes," she breathed. "To hear his daughter talk about Mr. Von Tussel having trouble... just like the rest of us. It was," she put her free hand across her heart, "inspirational."

"I'm so glad to hear it," I said, caught up in her enthusiasm.

"Oh, and don't worry about not setting up the author thing."

I stared at her. "What do you mean?"

"You know, the students taking Mr. Von Tussel around."

"I did recommend you to the organizer," I said, slowly.

She looked confused. "Dr. Raleigh said you were organizing everything."

"That's not true. There must have been a mix up. I'm sorry it didn't work out." I fought to keep my tone even, countering a sudden surge of anger at Simone.

"It's all good," Keandra said, tossing her braids over her shoulders. "I went up and talked to Mina after the workshop." Her dark eyes glowed with admiration. "She offered to introduce me to Mr. Von Tussel on Saturday after the reading."

"Wonderful. Hope you enjoy it."

"Thank you," she said. "Have a good night, Dr. Maclean."

As she wandered away, Nate turned to me. "What was that about Simone?"

"Oh," I said, choosing my words carefully since I was in a group. "There was a miscommunication about organizing the volunteers to help Damon while he was visiting."

Across the table, Francisco snorted. "That's not what Simone said." He raked his hand through his hair, grabbed the beer just placed in front of him, and took a long swig.

"What do you mean?" I asked, unsure if I wanted to hear the answer.

"She said you were in charge but just blew it off."

My stomach lurched. I should have known Simone was setting me up. At first, I thought she was just passing the responsibility buck because she forgot or something, but now I understood she was blaming me to anyone who would listen.

I shook my head, my lips pressed tight.

"You weren't in charge?" He stared at me.

"No. Simone came up to me at the library after our planning meeting and offered to handle everything."

"Well, that's not what she's saying now."

"Actually—" I saw no way around it. I had to give them the rundown of the whole Simone saga. Or at least a general outline.

Because she was messing with my reputation now, which I needed to protect if I wanted to stay at Stonedale University. And I did.

Francisco might understand, given what he'd gone through with Jasper. Heck, he might even have some pointers for navigating the situation.

Calista, next to Francisco, looked expectantly at me.

"What I'm about to say has to stay just among the four of us, okay? Because I will name multiple ways in which Simone Raleigh has tried to sabotage me. She's evil."

Calista's eyes widened and her body made an awkward jolt, which culminated in her pointing with her chin to the space beside me.

Because of course that's where Simone was standing.

She didn't look at me as she addressed the table. "Just thought I'd come over and say hello. I'm here with Chancellor Wellington and my mother, who flew in for the weekend." She gestured toward another booth across the room, where the chancellor was chatting with a blonde woman in an obviously expensive suit with a circle of colossal pearls around her neck.

The chancellor at a pub? I admired his willingness to mingle with the common people.

Then again, it wasn't as though there were many restaurants in Stonedale. I'd heard this one had excellent food too, so maybe that played a factor.

"The chancellor owns this restaurant," Simone continued, as if reading my thoughts. "Did you know that?"

I focused my eyes on the drink in front of me. I'd gotten a Diet Coke but now wished I'd chosen something with a kick. The chancellor owned this place? Hmmm. I'd assumed "Peak" in the restaurant title referred to nearby Pikes Peak, but perhaps it was a subtle reference to the chancellor's vantage point in the power hierarchy of Stonedale.

"So, Lila," Simone said, her tone carefully modulated. "You were saying something?"

"What?"

I could play innocent too. My cheeks burned though as I met her gaze.

"Yes, you were saying something about me. I gather you are unhappy. Perhaps I could share some thoughts?" I could only imagine what would happen if I stepped aside and let her narrate our adventures to date.

"Perhaps," I said, through clenched teeth, "for the time being, we could address the volunteer issue."

Her face took on a sympathetic cast. "Yes, it was really too bad you dropped the ball on that. I know the students were disappointed."

Beneath the table, my hands tightened into fists. I counted to five—I couldn't make it to ten—and responded as coolly as I could manage. "Simone, we both know you offered to organize the students, so it's very unfair of you to inform everyone otherwise."

Simone tittered—there was no other word for her tinkling, condescending laugh—and looked around the table to enlist support. No one moved.

"You were in the meeting, right? I never volunteered to take on the responsibility."

"No," I agreed. "You came up to me at the library the next day and told me you would handle it."

She tittered again. "I don't think so."

"Don't, Simone," I said grimly. "Enough of this."

She smoothed her shining blonde hair back and arranged her mouth into an amused smile. "I don't know what you're talking about, Lila. It's not even that big of a deal. Everything's been sorted out. Just admit your mistake, and we can all move on. My goodness, what a fuss." She sounded like a prim relative who had been called in to remedy an etiquette lapse.

A server brought a large silver tray. Simone stepped away to allow her to deliver our entrees. As the others picked up their silverware, she moved in right next to me, lowering her voice. "By the way Lila, Stephanie Barnes is very upset."

"Oh. Is everything okay?"

"Silly me. I said that wrong." Simone produced her tinkly laugh again. "Let me try again. She's upset with *you*." Simone leaned closer and hissed into my ear. "Because you accused her of plagiarism."

I leaned away until she stood up again.

"She's a darling student," Simone said, reverting to her usual chirpy style. "From an awfully good family. Her uncle has donated oodles of money to the football team."

"And?"

I understood the implication, but I wasn't about to give in.

"Maybe you could give her another chance. Let her rewrite the paper." The way she cocked her head was oddly birdlike.

"It's not going to happen, Simone," I said firmly. "Stephanie cheated. End of story."

She gave me an adorable pout. "I'm terribly sorry you feel that way. I guess I'll have to advise her to fill out a complaint after all."

A complaint would certainly make an unwelcome addition to my official file. But right is right. I couldn't—make that *wouldn't*—give in to blackmail, however politely it was worded.

I met her cold blue eyes. "Do what you have to do, Simone."

"You can't say I didn't try to help you, Lila," she said sadly, wrinkling her perfect nose and patting my shoulder.

It took all of my power not to swat away her elegant hands.

After she walked away, I put my hands on the table and took several deep breaths. The table was silent for a long moment.

"She's kind of a piece of work, isn't she?" Calista said. I wanted to hug her, but I settled for smiling appreciatively across the table. Francisco shot her a look and she rolled her eyes. "C'mon Fran. She's a liar."

"She lied about organizing the students, yes. And did you hear her just now?" I asked, so angry I was almost yelling.

"No. What did she say? And Lila..." Calista patted the air to indicate that I should take my volume down a notch.

"She encouraged someone to put in a student complaint against me."

"She what?" My cousin put down her fork. "Why?"

"The student plagiarized and didn't receive any credit for the assignment. Simone was pushing me to allow a rewrite, and I refused. Then she said the uncle of the student is a big donor, as if that makes a difference. And she's probably going to report all of it to the chancellor right now," I said, glancing across the room at their table.

"That's ridiculous," Nate said.

"Absurd," Calista agreed.

Francisco just shrugged.

Then Calista did the most surprising thing: she threw her arms around him and kissed his cheek. "Babe, you have got to snap out of this funk."

Babe?

I looked at Nate in surprise, then back to the couple now snuggling across the table from us. Francisco's smile changed his whole face—he looked years younger. And happier.

"You're together?" I pointed, moving my finger back and forth between them. "How did I not know this?"

Calista grinned at me. "We've been keeping it on the down low. But we've been together since the week after New Year's. Was that it?" She glanced at him for corroboration. "We bumped into each other at the grocery store after I came home from New York. We got to talking and decided to go to a movie we both wanted to see, and that's when it all began."

Francisco's gaze softened when he looked at her.

"Well," I said, turning to Nate, "first Mina and Jasper, now those two. Are we the only single people left on campus?"

"But Nate's not single either," said Calista, beaming at him.

I looked into Nate's eyes, stunned. "You're not?"

"No," he said, looking away.

"Lila doesn't know about..." asked Calista, sounding surprised.

"No," he said. "It never came up."

"Whatever," I said, though my heart raced as I willed him not to say he was seeing Simone.

"I'm dating Amanda Prescott." Nate said—shyly, it seemed. "She teaches in Fort Collins. We broke up for a while, but we're back together."

"Nice," I said automatically. "That's really...nice."

"She was on a Fulbright last year," Nate said. "In France. Just got back last week."

"Oh." I said. My mind was busily trying to assimilate the unexpected information. Suddenly, I had become the only single person at the table. Not that there was anything wrong with that.

"Will she be coming to visit soon?" Calista asked. "I haven't seen her in ages."

"She'll be here for the reading," Nate turned to me. "And you can meet her then."

"Sure."

"Maybe we could go out for drinks afterwards and you could get to know her," Calista said. "You'll love her. Everyone does."

Awesome.

Chapter 13

As I prepared for bed that evening, I thought about Nate's revelation. I ripped back the purple down blanket so hard it flew off the end of the bed. I sighed and walked around to reposition it. I didn't understand why I felt so irritated with him for not telling me about having a girlfriend.

Maybe because he didn't tell me until now.

Maybe because he didn't tell me until Calista practically forced him to.

Maybe because he kissed me last semester *and* didn't tell me.

I shook the thought out of my head. It wasn't all up to him. I could have made it a point to talk to him about the kiss, and I hadn't. I'd just let it linger there unaddressed, uncertain of its meaning. Sometimes talking about things made for awkwardness, and I definitely didn't want to risk losing our friendship.

I smoothed down the blanket and removed the cheerful lavender, yellow, and red suzani accent pillows, stacking them neatly on the window seat.

It was decided, then. I would never mention it. And he could enjoy his life with Ms. Fulbright Scholar.

I climbed into bed and opened up the paranormal mystery I'd borrowed from the library. It was all about a teacher who takes a position at a secluded boarding school and discovers that some of the other faculty members are secretly monsters of one kind or another.

One didn't need to go too far into the symbolism to understand the satisfying parallels in that.

Saturday night, I was back on campus, almost to the doors of Brynson. I'd slept in for the first time in forever, and the extra slumber had done wonders. I was even looking forward to the reading. I wondered which version of Damon we'd see tonight: the calm, charismatic literary lion or the exasperated grouch who might yell—or disappear—at any moment?

The hall was filled with people chatting in groups. I edged around them and went into the auditorium, hoping to find a good seat. At the bottom of the main aisle's gentle slope, I came upon Gilles Valmont and Alonzo Ferrara leaning against the stage talking.

"Hi, Lila," Gilles said. "Care to sit with us?"

I had hoped to find Calista, but she was probably with Francisco anyway. I didn't want to intrude.

"Sure," I said. "Thank you."

He gestured in his oily way toward two seats in the front row, close to the center aisle, where they had placed their coats. I put my own coat over the empty seat nearest me and turned back to face them.

"We were just talking about finally seeing Mr. Von Tussel in person," he said. "Neither of us have been to one of his events before."

"I'm psyched," said Alonzo, flushing. That was easy enough to guess from his gleeful face. His brown jacket hung loosely on him, as if he had borrowed his father's suit for a special occasion. "And tweeting about it."

I smiled at him.

"I hope we get to meet him." Alonzo added.

"We should try, though it might be hard to get access to him," Gilles said. "According to Jasper, Damon is going to announce something important—"

"Speak of the devil," said Alonzo.

Jasper strode down the aisle confidently as always. His gelled blond hair looked sharp enough to cut glass. He saluted us jauntily and pulled himself up onto the stage, looking around the room for a moment before squatting down and perching on the edge. I noticed he tended to position himself higher than others in the room, if at all possible. Echoes of the chancellor.

"What was that about a big announcement?" I asked Gilles.

"I don't know," he said slowly. "Jasper mentioned—"

A coughing fit covered Gilles's next words. Jasper stopped coughing and shot him a warning look. "I don't know what the announcement is either," he said loudly. "I guess we'll all find out tonight."

"Where's Mina?" I asked him.

"She's backstage with Damon, the chancellor, and Tally. You know his agent, right?"

We all nodded.

"How's Damon doing? Is he nervous?" I asked.

"He's terrific. We spent the day together," said Jasper. The two scholars visibly deflated at that. "Mina said he *was* nervous about the reading—though he would never admit such a thing to me—so we tried to keep his mind off of it. We went to the Denver Art Museum for most of the day, then had a quick dinner here in town at the place with the..." He traced a half-circle in the air with his finger.

"Silver's?" I guessed. Silver's was a popular Stonedale restaurant. All bright light and ferns, it also had an outdoor patio surrounded by a rock fence with a number of arches decorating its upper half.

He snapped his fingers. "That's it. Yes. Great food." He paused for a moment as if savoring the deliciousness. "We talked about his new book," he added casually, for the benefit of Gilles and Alonzo. They were obviously hungry for more information, hanging on his every word.

"He's going to read from it tonight, right?" asked Alonzo.

"Of course. He doesn't read from *The Medusa Variation* anymore," Jasper said.

"Right, right," said Alonzo, typing on his cell phone distractedly. Tweeting again, no doubt.

"He asked me for input," said Jasper, attempting and failing to sound modest.

"Cool," said Alonzo. "Can you give us any hints?"

"You'll have to wait and see, bro," Jasper said to him. Then he addressed me. "Anyway, we came early so he'd have time to get situated before the reading."

Gilles remained quiet. He looked, if I had to put a word on it, resentful. Scholars were extremely protective of their topics. It had to be difficult to have to compete with another scholar who has the inside track to your author. And now Jasper was about as "inside" as it got—before too long, he would be Damon's son-in-law. Gilles and Alonzo hadn't even met Damon. Not that meeting your author was necessary to write well about them. But when you spend so much time and effort honoring the work of an individual, you can't help but be interested in them. I could understand why they might be jealous of Jasper.

"I'd better go find them," said Jasper, turning to me. "Have you seen Francisco? He was supposed to meet us. I already took Damon backstage because I didn't know what else to do."

"Sorry. I haven't. I could call him if you like."

"No, I have his number," said Jasper. "I'll just go take a look around outside first."

As he hopped down and hurried up the aisle, I noticed the room was filling quickly. We all took our seats and settled in. The energy of the crowd was soothing, I thought, letting it wash over me. All of these people intrigued by books and the power of words— this was my tribe. From where we were sitting, I could see Tally and Mina waiting in the wings with Damon. It was almost time.

Just before seven, two men in green Stonedale Facilities uniforms went up on stage and relocated the wooden lectern with the crimson-and-silver crest on the front. Hopefully that would foil any catwalk-attack plots. Fingers crossed. Finally, the house lights lowered and the crowd fell silent. Francisco walked out from the wings and stood at the lectern, his glasses reflecting the spotlight for a moment when he looked out over the audience. He looked calm and polished in a blue suit, white shirt, and turquoise bolo tie, but I wondered if he was nervous after his last time onstage. I half-expected him to crane his neck toward the catwalk above, just to make sure nothing was about to plummet downward, but he kept focused on the page in front of him.

"Welcome," he said, "to a very special event. I'm Francisco de Francisco, an assistant professor in the department of English. Before I introduce our guest speaker, please allow me to present Chancellor Wellington, who would like to say a few words."

The chancellor never missed a chance to sprinkle a few bon mots and elicit donations. He strode out on the stage, stepped up to the lectern, and spoke in a hearty, commanding voice. "Ladies and Gentlemen, thank you for attending this event in our popular Twenty-First Century Arts and Culture Series. We here at Stonedale University strive to serve the community by bringing an array of esteemed writers, artists, and other performers to campus. Such activities are made available of course by your generous support—"

I tuned him out, taking the opportunity to scan the crowd for my colleagues. It was too dark to make out facial features, so I wheeled back around, defeated.

He relinquished the microphone to a polite round of applause, and Francisco stepped back into the spotlight. "It's my honor to introduce to you a man who, quite single-handedly, changed literary history. His first book, *The Medusa Variation*, was a brave and insightful novel about the price of war. It was a bestseller and won numerous literary prizes. His latest book, *In Medias Res*, came out last year to great acclaim. It has been on top ten lists of all kinds around the world. Critics are already discussing the new literary form demonstrated by this latest effort—a collection of stories without beginning or endings. The author has discussed these pieces as 'medions,' or literary catapults, stories intended to force you into an active listening mode. We are most honored to have him here tonight to read and discuss some of his work with you. Please join me in welcoming award-winning author Damon Von Tussel."

Francisco initiated the applause by clapping gently. He turned to his left, where Damon was moving slowly across the stage, his white beard centered between the lapels of the black coat he wore over a blue dress shirt and black trousers. The tapping of his mahogany cane on the stage echoed through the room, and I felt almost mesmerized by the sound. He seemed to weave at one point, and Francisco quickly went to his side—presumably to hand Damon the book from which he would be reading, but perhaps also to steady him. A few steps later, Damon paused, looking confused, and Francisco whispered to him. He nodded and, finally, Damon reached the lectern and gripped it tightly, hanging the cane carefully on the right side. That was strange. I was used to seeing Damon blast through the world like a rocket.

He reached inside his jacket and pulled out his reading glasses, which he unfolded and settled on his nose. He sniffed. He opened the book, deliberately turning pages until he reached the one he wanted. He laughed to himself, then looked out at the audience and covered his mouth as if he'd said something shocking.

"Evenin'," he said, his upper lip moving around the word as if it were unfamiliar.

All signs pointed to the likelihood that Damon Von Tussel was very, very drunk.

I saw Francisco hovering on the edge of the stage. He must have come to the same conclusion I had: our guest speaker was hammered.

Damon looked down for a long moment before leaning toward the microphone. "S'nice," he said, elongating the "s" in a decided slur.

Then he pitched forward onto the wooden lectern, smashed his head, and slid backwards, in an obscenely slow manner, onto the floor.

"Dad!" Mina shrieked from the wings and ran toward her father. Her clogs thundered on the stage, and the hem of her long black dress trailed dramatically behind her. It was as impressive as watching one of the Furies fly across the room. Kneeling next to Damon, Mina tried to revive her father, patting his face wildly and crooning to him. Then she screamed at Jasper, who had followed her, "Call 911! Now!"

Francisco was already dialing.

Chapter 14

An hour later, order had been restored. The chancellor had informed the audience he was truly sorry about "the setback." He had said this event—"or an equally prestigious one"—would be rescheduled for a future date. Everyone should check the university website for more information.

The audience had dissipated almost instantly at the request of the police, who had responded to the 911 call very quickly.

Damon and Mina had been whisked away by the ambulance, sirens flashing. That sound was ominous, as always, and those of us left behind were decidedly out of sorts.

"That's the second person who has been carried off this stage this week," Francisco said glumly. "What is going on around here?"

"I know," said Calista somberly. "It's like we're cursed." She absentmindedly readjusted the pale peach fringed scarf she wore over her black wool dress.

"Don't say that," I said soothingly. "Damon just had too much to drink."

Francisco snorted. "Probably should've seen it coming. He's a notorious drunk."

"You mean he's an alcoholic," corrected Calista. "He can't help it. It's a disease, you know."

"Well, he needs help," said Francisco.

I was overwhelmed by a sudden sense of déjà vu. Here we were, waiting to be dismissed once again after an interrupted event, only this time we sat in the back row of the empty auditorium.

The door swung open and Jasper rushed in. "I need to go over to the hospital," he said. "Can one of you drive me? We walked here, and the ambulance people wouldn't let me ride with them." It was the first time I'd ever seen him even slightly discombobulated.

"I'll take you," said Francisco, surprising me. He stood up. "Do they know what's going on?"

"He passed out is all I know," said Jasper, practically vibrating. You could tell he wanted to leave instantly.

"He seemed incredibly drunk." Calista said.

"I know," said Jasper. "When I left him before the reading, though, I hadn't seen him take a drink all day."

"That doesn't mean he wasn't drinking all day," muttered Francisco.

"Shh," whispered Calista.

Francisco gave Calista a quick kiss and said goodbye to me, then followed Jasper out of the building.

Maybe the two men would have a chance to bond. I hoped so. Francisco had been miserable for a long time because of the tension between them. I didn't know how Jasper felt about it, but perhaps a peace treaty could be negotiated.

"Should we try to go over there too?" Calista said, sounding not quite convinced about the idea.

"I don't think so. Maybe we could visit tomorrow morning, once we know what's happening. They'll probably give Damon an IV and let him sleep it off, if it's too much alcohol."

"I hope he doesn't have alcohol poisoning," Calista said quietly. "One of my friends died from it at school."

"That's horrible," I said, my breath catching in my throat.

"It was very sad. He was only nineteen," she said, tearing up. "A fraternity initiation. You hear those stories all the time. Well, they're true."

"I'm so sorry." I couldn't hug her, given the awkward positioning of our seats. I settled for patting her arm.

"All I can do now is try to warn my students about that sort of thing."

"That's good, Cal."

"I think most of them ignore me. You know how some students think they know everything?"

"Some professors think that too," I said.

She made a sound which was half-laugh, half-sob—her eyes glistening in the dim light of the auditorium.

The same Campus Security person we'd spoken to after the panel—Officer Stanley—trudged over to where we were sitting. His mustache was even more unruly than last time. "Do you need any additional assistance, ladies?"

"No, we were just waiting to see if you needed anything from us," I said.

He returned my smile. "Thanks for waiting, but we're going to lock up."

"Did you find anything strange? I know the accident earlier this week turned out to have a mysterious origin."

His lips tightened. Apparently he wasn't going to share any information with a regular old civilian.

"You can tell us," I encouraged. "We're on the Arts Week planning committee." I was making it sound as though membership was akin to being on the Council of Overlords or something, but I hoped that an appeal to authority might coax information out of him.

He considered this for a moment. "Nothing strange," he said finally.

I pulled one of my Stonedale business cards from my wallet and handed it to him. "If you think of anything, would you please call me?"

Clearly humoring me, Officer Stanley tucked it carefully into his breast pocket and patted it. Then he pointed toward the door, inviting us to clear out.

Outside, the cold air felt like a slap in the face. I shivered and was buttoning up my coat when my cell phone rang. After fumbling in my bag for a moment, I finally located it and checked the screen.

"It's my mother," I said to Calista. "Can you wait one sec?"

She nodded, pulling out her phone. "I'll check in with Fran."

I clicked the accept button, and my mother's voice poured out.

"How did the reading go? It was tonight, right?"

"It didn't happen," I said. "Damon passed out onstage."

"Passed out? Is he okay?" She sounded so upset that I wondered if she still had feelings for him.

"I don't know anything yet, but I'll let you know as soon as I do."

"Where is he right now?" she persisted.

"At the hospital. Mom, he was just really drunk. It's probably not a big deal."

"He never drinks before a reading, Lila," my mother reproached me. "It's the one thing he is absolutely serious about."

"I don't know," I said. "Maybe he was just really nervous about this one for some reason and broke his rule. He didn't show up at the workshop yesterday either."

There was silence on the other end of the line. I could imagine my mother's lovely face pondering the situation. She was probably twirling one of her red curls as she did so. I'd seen her do that a thousand times while surveying one of her art projects in process.

"You know what? I'm coming out there. I'll grab the next flight."

I gasped. "No, Mom, you don't need to. Really."

"It sounds like Damon is in trouble. I may be able to help. I should have come out there anyway, to support you."

"My part in the events is already over, Mom. Honestly, you don't have to—"

"I'll see you tomorrow, Lila," she said. "Love you." My phone beeped to indicate she'd hung up.

I turned to Calista, who was checking something on her phone. She looked up with an inquisitive expression.

"So Mom's coming out to Stonedale," I said.

Her face lit up. "When? For what?"

"Tomorrow. To help Damon, she said, but I don't know how she can do that, exactly."

"Can't wait to see Aunt Vi."

I wasn't sure what my mother's plans were, but clearly she was worried about Damon. She also loved to immerse herself in drama. Maybe she wanted him back. Now there was a dreadful thought. I hoped I'd be able to keep everything from turning into the Violet and Damon Reunited Tour.

"Do you want to grab a coffee? I don't feel like going home yet." Calista looked at an exquisite gold watch on her slim wrist. "It's just after eight."

"Sure," I said. If anything, I could use the warmth.

"Let's go to Scarlett's," she said.

"Sounds perfect." It was within a few blocks of both our homes. She texted Francisco and we started walking east. As we passed through the main gates of Stonedale, she patted the head of the stone gryphon.

"What are you doing?"

"It's for good luck. Ooh, it's freezing though." She shoved her hand back into her coat pocket.

"Wow, there are a lot of good luck rituals around here. Last fall, Nate made me plunge my hand into the fountain in the middle of campus for luck."

She laughed. "I think we all probably feel we can use as much luck as we can gather. You should pat the gryphon too."

"I'm not going to—"

"Pat the gryphon, Lil," she commanded sternly.

I backed up and rested my hand on top of the statue. An icy sensation flowed up my arm, and my teeth began to chatter.

"Oh my gosh, look at you," said Calista. "Let's run to Scarlett's."

A few blocks later, we arrived at the recognizable awning outside of the café. Another patron walked out of the red wooden door and held it for us. We tramped inside, slightly breathless, and I felt immediately better to be among the chattering crowd seated at the small tables dotting the room. Scarlett's red and gold decor was welcoming, as usual. The barista took our order: a decaf latte for me and a mocha for Calista.

"Want to split a chocolate muffin?" Calista glanced at me. "We just went running, after all."

"Sure," I said. "Though I don't know if it counts as 'running,' technically."

"It's as close as I get to it lately."

The cashier took our money and we moved to the end of the counter to wait for our drinks. Calista's phone chirped and she looked down to read a text. I gazed at the framed vintage photos on the walls depicting various citizens of Stonedale at work.

"That was Fran," Calista said. "He's going to join us. Before he gets here, tell me the truth: what do you think of him?"

"He seems nice," I said. "I was impressed with his paper at the panel. He's a wonderful speaker."

"And quite fetching as well." She blushed. "Those blue eyes...mmm."

"He is very attractive," I agreed.

"The blue comes from his father, he said, who is Italian. Did you know that?"

"I did not," I said. "But his last name was originally Franco, right? So that would make sense."

"Yes. Sorry. I know I sound like a teenager."

"It's fine. As long as you're happy. You are, right?"

She sighed. "Deliriously."

"That's great, Cal. You deserve it."

"Now we need to find someone for you—" she began, pausing when her message tone sounded.

I sent up a small thanks to the powers that be for interrupting us at precisely that moment. As she picked up her phone, I caught sight of Gilles and Alonzo sitting in the back of the café. Their heads were close together and they were talking intently. Calista was texting again, so I told her I'd be back in a minute and headed toward the scholars.

When I got close to the table, Gilles saw me and smoothly straightened up.

"Lila. What a surprise. Join us?" It seemed unnecessarily loud—in fact, several people at neighboring tables looked up, startled. Was he trying to warn his companion of my presence?

"Thanks, but I'm here with my cousin," I said. "Just wanted to say hello. How are you guys doing?"

Their eyes met, as if they were agreeing on something.

"We're fine, but we're worried about Damon," Alonzo said, blinking rapidly. His Adam's apple bobbed up and down in concert.

"Any news?" Gilles stared at me while adjusting his glasses for the millionth time since I met him. I didn't know if it was a fit issue or a tic.

"Nothing yet. Hey, did you guys see anything weird at the reading?"

"Like what?" Alonzo asked, taking a sip of coffee.

"I don't know. Anything seem odd about Damon when he first came out on stage?"

"You mean aside from him being too drunk to stand up?" Alonzo said glumly.

"We don't know what happened to him," Gilles replied quickly. "He might have had a medical issue."

"Or he might have been sloshed," Alonzo insisted.

That was the most likely answer, but I pressed on anyway. "How about otherwise? Any people acting strange in the audience? Or someone you didn't think should be in the wings?"

They looked at each other again, as if reaching another silent agreement, then shook their heads.

What were they not saying? I thought back too, trying to slow the memory down, but came up empty.

"Lila? Hello?"

Gilles was waving a white paper napkin at me.

"Sorry," I said. "What did you say?"

"Have you seen Jasper or Francisco around?" Gilles asked.

"No," I said.

An uncomfortable silence descended, during which Gilles folded and refolded his napkin into precise, ever-smaller squares.

"Well, have a good night," Alonzo said finally, which I took as my cue to leave.

Back in the waiting zone with Calista, I glanced over at the men. They had leaned toward each other again and were speaking rapidly—this time with additional gesticulations. I didn't know what had them all fired up, but they certainly didn't want to share it with me. I couldn't imagine what in our brief conversation had fueled the fire.

Our drinks arrived, and we carried them over to a table that had just opened up near the window. I slid into the booth facing the side wall so Calista could keep an eye out for Francisco coming through the front door. Once we were settled in, we both wrapped our hands around the large mugs.

"Ah," said Calista happily. "I don't even have to drink it to be happy. Just the warmth and the smell are heavenly."

"It's nice to be in a place where things seem so normal after the past few days."

"I meant to ask if you were feeling better about the reading." Her gray eyes studied me with concern.

"Well, I have to admit, it was pretty awful to see Damon slide down the lectern like that."

"You were front and center, weren't you?"

"Yes. Where were you?"

"I was on the left near the front. Francisco had to go onstage, so we sat on the side. I thought it was odd when he didn't come back to sit with me after introducing Damon. He must have sensed that something was wrong." She tilted her head slightly and regarded the steam coming off of her mocha.

"I think you're right. From where I was sitting, I could see him edge out of the wings, like he was anxious about Damon being onstage alone."

I blew on my latte and took a sip. It was the perfect temperature.

"Hey, did you happen to see that Alonzo and Gilles are here?" I asked, pointing to the back as unobtrusively as I could.

She twisted around, then leaned out of the booth almost horizontally to get a better vantage point.

"Calista, could you please be more casual about it?" I begged her.

She hoisted herself back upright and rolled her eyes. "How am I supposed to see them if I can't look?"

"You can look but maybe don't fall out of the booth while you're doing it?"

"I give up," she said. "I take your word for it that they're here. Why?"

"Well, they were acting peculiar," I said.

"How?"

"They were whispering up a storm, but when I got over there, they stopped. Like they didn't want me to hear them."

"So maybe they didn't want you to hear them," she said, shrugging.

"It seemed like more than that," I protested.

"Maybe they were gossiping," she said.

"It seemed like more than that too."

"How?"

"I don't know. Just seemed suspicious."

She grinned. "Lila Maclean, Girl Detective."

"What's that supposed to mean?"

"Well, ever since last semester, you've had your clue antennae up. Everything seems suspicious to you these days."

"Because things keep on *happening*."

She reached out and touched my hand, a contrite expression on her face. "You're right. And I was just kidding, Lil. I do appreciate your new mindset. Skill set. Whatever it is."

Truth was I didn't know why I was distrustful of Gilles and Alonzo. I had exactly zero evidence the professors were involved in any of this, other than all that frenzied whispering.

"Hey all," Francisco greeted us. I hadn't even heard him

approach us, with all the background noise: the grinder ran every two minutes, and the bells on the back of the door jingled almost as often. Normally, it didn't seem quite as loud as it did tonight. Maybe I was just jumpy.

He scooted in next to Calista and kissed her cheek as he peeled off his coat. Now that their relationship was public knowledge, they greeted each other that way as often as possible. It was adorable, I had to admit. Even if it made me feel like a third wheel. But I was happy for them.

To give them some privacy, I looked out the window at the sidewalk glistening in the light of the streetlamp. Small hearts painted along the bottom half of the glass drew my attention, reminding me that Valentine's Day was fast approaching.

At least we hadn't run into Nate and Amanda tonight.

Chapter 15

"Lila Maclean," said a deep voice beside me. I looked up to see Detective Lexington Archer of the Stonedale PD smiling down at me. However, instead of his usual suit, he was wearing a gray flannel shirt and jeans. The blue tee underneath pulled tight across his sizeable muscles and matched his eyes nicely.

"Hi, Detective Archer," I said.

"Call me Lex."

That was a surprise. Last fall, most of our encounters had involved him grilling me about one crime or another. Not sure what warranted the slide into first-name basis, but I wasn't going to object. "Hi, Lex. What are you doing here?"

He held up a book and a mug. "I come here to read sometimes. And they have pretty great coffee."

That also surprised me. He didn't seem like a book-and-café kind of person.

"Yes, the drinks are good." I invited him to join us, expecting him to decline.

"Thanks," he said quickly, sliding into the booth beside me. He still wore his dark hair in the same buzz cut he'd had last fall. He was an all-around no-nonsense guy.

We made small talk until, across the table, the lovebirds had concluded their nuzzling, then I introduced the detective to Francisco. They shook hands.

Calista looked thrilled to see him. I couldn't imagine why. Last semester, he'd carted her off to jail.

We filled him in on the events of the week—the threatening email, the manuscript theft, Jasper's concussion—and explained that Francisco had just arrived from the hospital, where Damon had been taken.

The detective gave his head a little shake. "That school of yours is something else. Any idea who might have a grudge?"

I shrugged. "I wish I knew."

Calista looked at Francisco. "How are you doing, babe?"

"Not great," he said, letting out a long breath slowly, obviously trying to let go of some of the stress of the evening.

"Do you want something to drink? Or do you want some of my mocha?" She pushed the mug closer to him.

He waved it away.

"So what happened? Is Damon okay? Is Jasper okay? How's Mina holding up?"

At his look, she fell quiet. He took off his glasses and cleaned them on his shirt as he spoke. "Damon was drugged."

Calista swatted her boyfriend on the arm. "That's not funny, Fran."

"It's true," he said, holding the glasses up to the light before putting them back on. "They were telling Mina when we walked into the room. Damon's blood test detected benzodiazepine. Not a huge dose, but enough to slow a guy his size down for awhile."

"What's benzodiazepine?" my cousin asked him.

"Benzos are anti-anxiety meds. Xanax, Ativan, and so on."

"But why would someone drug him?" Calista stared at Francisco.

"Who knows? It's a pretty sick thing to do, in my opinion," he said. "And it could have ended up even worse for him."

"What do you mean?" I asked.

"The drug shouldn't be combined with alcohol," he said. "Which Damon tends to have in his system—I think that's been pretty well established. Could have been fatal."

"What a tragedy it would have been," said Calista.

"Yes," I agreed.

We all sat silently for a moment, processing.

"Why did they let him go onstage if he was acting strange?" Calista leaned forward slightly.

Francisco shrugged. "Maybe it didn't hit him fully until he was at the lectern. So much depends on the size of the dose, how much he drank, and when he drank it. He could have chugged down half of the cup right before he went onstage."

"You'd think it would have been obvious," my cousin continued, unwilling to move on just yet.

"Mina did say he didn't seem like himself, but she thought it was just a bad case of stage fright, which he apparently gets sometimes, and Tally seems pretty oblivious in general," Francisco said.

"Does he take medication for his anxiety? Maybe he just took too much?"

Francisco shook his head. "No, they talked about that possibility. He doesn't have a prescription."

Lex cleared his throat. "Do you know if they're keeping him overnight for observation or sending him home? That would give us an idea of the severity of the issue."

"I don't know," said Francisco slowly. "Maybe I should follow up. Do you happen to know the number of the hospital? I'll try Jasper if the nurses won't tell me anything."

The detective reeled it off the top of his head. Francisco slid out of the booth and walked outside the café.

"Babe! Your coat," Calista called after him. But the door had already closed behind him. She picked up her mocha and took a sip. "So Detective Archer—" she began.

"Lex, please," he interjected.

Her smile grew wider. "Lex. Are you married?"

I shook my head slightly, but she ignored me.

"Nope," he said. He smiled pleasantly at her and took a sip of his coffee.

"Do you have a significant other?"

He took another drink. "Nope."

If she asked another question, I would have to hide under the table to conceal my telltale flush. She was so obviously trying to fix us up.

"Do you have plans for Valentine's Day?" she said, glancing pointedly at me. Okay, that was it. Game over. I mumbled something about having to make a call and began grabbing blindly for my phone.

Only I knocked over Lex's coffee instead.

"I'm so sorry," I gushed as the pool of hot liquid rained down on our legs. "I was just trying to find my phone."

"In my coffee cup?" he said, grinning.

"Yeah, um. Sorry."

"Don't worry about it," he said. "But some might call that a Freudian slip."

I paused in the act of mopping up the spill with the pile of napkins I'd pulled frantically from the silver holder on the table. "What do you mean?"

"Well," he said, "You probably have some residual anger about our encounters last fall."

"Now that you mention it, all those suspicious looks were getting tiresome."

He laughed. Thank goodness. "Just doing my job," he said. "You are walking the straight and narrow this semester, Professor?"

"Yes, Officer."

I batted my eyelashes.

"Lex," he reminded me. "Just think of me as your friendly neighborhood detective."

"Not so friendly last semester," I muttered.

He grinned.

I had to admit, I liked this side of Detective Archer.

"Sorry again about the spill," I said. "May I buy you another coffee? Or a new pair of pants? Or both?"

Lex laughed. "No to all of those, thanks."

"Moving on," Calista interjected. "The reason I was asking about Valentine's Day is because we are going to a reception at the chancellor's mansion. Should be swanky. Would you like to join us?"

"The reception will go on even if Von Tussel isn't willing or able to attend?" Lex seemed faintly disturbed.

"Oh yes," Francisco said, returning to the booth. "The chancellor has spent a lot of money on this party. And get this: they've already rescheduled the reading for next Friday too, according to Campus Security, who are less than delighted at facing another public event on the Brynson Hall stage this month. Let's just hope the old things-happen-in-threes rule doesn't apply here."

"We'll be sure to have a Stonedale PD presence there too," Lex said. "Given what's happened already."

Francisco thanked him.

"But what if Damon bails?" asked Calista, voicing the same thing I'd just been pondering. "I probably would, if someone drugged me."

"Then they'll have another author read instead," said Francisco. He did a fair imitation of Spencer's intonation at the planning committee meeting: "The event *will* take place."

"How long does it take someone to recover from something like that?" Calista asked Lex.

"Depends on the amount ingested."

"They think he'll be able to attend the reception," Francisco confirmed.

"Lila, maybe you should check in with him tomorrow. Since you know him and everything," Calista said.

"I don't have his phone number," I said. "You do, right, Francisco?" He nodded.

"No, I meant you should go over to see him," my cousin said. "Ooh, maybe you should bring Aunt Vi. I'm sure seeing her would cheer him up."

"Cal, you know they didn't end things on a very good note," I reminded her. She was really on a fixing-people-up bend tonight. The joy from her own relationship was probably making her see red. In a romantic sense.

"But they still harbor a passion for each other. Everybody knows that," she told Lex. "I read it in *People*."

Francisco snorted.

"Are you snorting at the romantic part or the *People* part?" Calista demanded, staring in mock outrage at Francisco.

"Both," he said.

"Oh shush," she said, smacking his arm. "There's valuable information in that magazine, and if you weren't such a snob, you'd understand."

He rolled his eyes, but it was in a good-natured way. She clearly had him charmed. She turned her attention back to Lex. "Will you be able to join us for the reception, Detective?"

He gave me a sideways glance. "Are you sure I won't be intruding?"

"Of course not," Calista said. "We'd love your company."

At least she was making it sound like a group thing. Maybe Lex wouldn't think she was asking on my behalf.

"I think there may be a space on Lila's dance card," she added, as if we'd just magically been swept into a Jane Austen novel.

And there it was. Complete and utter mortification.

"There won't be much dancing," I informed his coffee cup because I couldn't bring myself to meet his eyes. "Just academics milling around in their formal wear, fancying themselves patrons of the arts. Honestly, you'll probably be bored to death."

"To death?" Lex said, his eyebrows raised. "Then you may *need* a detective. I accept."

"Good, then it's settled. Why don't you and Lila exchange numbers so you can iron out the details." Calista flashed me a meaningful look. "You probably don't still have it handy from last semester, right?"

I could hardly speak. I felt like a bride who had just been introduced to her groom in an arranged-marriage scenario. I knew Calista was trying to be kind, but it was all far too awkward.

"If you give me your number," Lex said quietly, "I'll call you tomorrow."

I did.

A few minutes later, we were standing out front. It was even colder now, and I couldn't help shivering. I didn't relish the walk home, but I was desperate to get away from Calista and her blatant matchmaking attempts.

"I'm going to take off," I said. "Thanks for the, uh, chat, all." I turned to go.

"Can I give you a ride?" asked Lex. Calista, standing behind him, did a brief happy dance. I ignored her.

"No, thank you."

"It's practically arctic out here. Please let me give you a ride," he said.

I didn't say anything for a minute, weighing the humiliation factor against the temperature. I shivered again, though it was more like a tremor this time.

"I insist," he said. "Don't make me flash my badge at you."

I accepted.

"Right this way," he said, pointing to a red Honda Civic parked on the sidewalk.

"I have an Accord," I announced for no apparent reason, then wondered what was wrong with me.

"Another Honda person?" he said. "I knew there was something I liked about you."

Relationships have been built on less.

Wait, why was I thinking about relationships? It must be the cold.

He unlocked the passenger side and held the door open.

I climbed inside. His car was very clean and smelled like coffee from the half-full takeout cup sitting in the center holder.

As Lex got into the car, the dome light reflected one silver strand in the top of his short, dark hair. For some reason, I liked that.

"Where to?"

"Just around the corner. Haven Street."

"Here we go."

He put the key into the ignition and turned it. Bach blared out of the speakers.

"Sorry," he said, twisting the volume knob.

My gaze fell on the coffee cup in the holder.

"You must really like coffee," I said, as he pulled out of the spot and headed down Main Street.

"What?"

"Well, you have a half of a cup in here but you went to Scarlett's to get more."

"Oh."

Something occurred to me suddenly. "Wait, did you know we were in there?"

He made a scoffing sound. "You think I was driving by and caught sight of you through the window, so I decided to park my car, grab a book, and pretend to bump into you?"

I didn't say anything.

"Wow. That's quite an assumption. I just like to read there sometimes."

"Ah." What else was there to say, really?

He turned onto my street. "Which one?"

I pointed to my tiny bungalow, and he stopped in front of it.

"Home sweet home," I said stupidly.

He gave my house the once-over. "Very nice. Shall I walk you to your door?"

It was a straight shot up the short sidewalk. "No thanks."

"Talk to you tomorrow, then," he said. "Pleasure running into you tonight."

"You too," I said.

"Even though you did basically accuse me of stalking you."

"That's not what I said exactly," I protested.

He nodded.

"Sorry." I was so embarrassed it was all I could do not to leap out of the car.

"Though I *might* have swerved my course a smidge," he continued, after a small beat. "After I saw you there."

I blinked at him. He did run into me on purpose?

"Now. Please go inside, so I can see you're safe."

I did so, turning to wave goodbye once I'd unlocked the door. As he drove away, I entertained the thought of spending time with Detective Lex Archer and found myself more than a little intrigued by the idea.

Chapter 16

Spencer had emailed us all, calling for an emergency planning meeting on Sunday at noon. Seemed like all of our planning meetings were emergencies. What a disaster Arts Week was turning out to be.

Calista texted me at quarter after eleven to ask if I wanted to walk over together. I messaged back a quick *Meet you there.* I was racing around preparing for my mother's first visit to Stonedale. She was taking a cab from the airport and would arrive at two. I'd spent the morning dusting, vacuuming, and washing linens. Since I didn't have a bed in the guest room—I used it as my office—she would have to sleep on my pull-out sofa. She might have preferred to stay in a hotel, order room service, and have her own space, but there wasn't a single available room in town because people had flown in from across the country just to hear Damon read. Sometimes I forgot how famous he really was.

My cell phone rang a moment later. Of course Calista would want to know why we couldn't go together. I hit the accept button without looking at the screen, informed her I couldn't talk, hit the off button, and threw my phone into my black satchel. I didn't have a minute to spare.

After making the foldaway bed up and taking the fastest shower in the universe, I wrestled my long damp hair into a ponytail, pulled on a black sweater and jeans, grabbed my bag and headed out to the ancient Accord parked in front of my house. I almost never drove to campus because I lived so close, but I'd be late for the meeting if I walked. I started the engine and waited for my trusty ride to warm up. Many were the days I wished for an attached garage like Calista had, but such was not the case. At least the sun had been out long enough this week that I didn't have to scrape the windshield free of ice. On-street parking was rough on windshields, what with all the snow and hail storms Colorado offered its residents, and a small crack was slowly inching its way across the glass. It would have to be replaced soon, though I wasn't certain the expense would be worth it, given the age of my car. A problem for another day, I told myself; right now, I have too much going on to deal with it.

Finally, the cold engine light went off, and I eased the car into drive. I stared at my house for a nanosecond, trying to anticipate how it would look through my mother's eyes. The pomegranate door against the gray paint and white trim looked cheerful, but maybe I needed a wreath of some kind. My mother would know just what to get, I was sure. Maybe I could beguile her into visiting the boutiques on Main Street if we had a minute. She could help me pick something out as a welcome gift for Glynnis, too.

The chancellor had organized a swift public relations campaign alerting interested parties that the reading had been rescheduled for next week. In addition to the website announcements and email blasts I'd seen earlier today, I now noticed yellow posters with Damon's face looking fiercely out from the center plastered everywhere as I drove to campus. I hoped it meant he was well on the mend at this point.

I parked in the lot closest to Crandall Hall. As I took the stairs three at a time, Glynnis gave me a warm greeting from the faculty library doorway. She was holding a stack of handouts and was clad in what looked like more vintage treasures—a fitted canary-colored jacket accessorized with multiple Bakelite bracelets. I ducked past her. Working on a weekend and sunnily too? Glynnis was indeed a gem. Spencer smiled at me as I dropped into a seat at the conference table. I was two minutes late, but he wasn't the kind of person who would make a big deal out of it. Thank goodness.

"Appreciate your coming, all." Spencer always extended gratitude, as if attendance was voluntary. It wasn't, but he was respectful in general about acknowledging us as professionals, which went a long way toward setting a positive tone in the department. "I'll try to keep this brief today, in light of the gathering this evening. I hope you will all be able to attend." Attendance was also mandatory for the chancellor's reception, at least for committee members. "Please remember the reading has been rescheduled for Friday evening. Mr. Von Tussel has kindly agreed to—"

"What happened to him, anyway?" asked Norton, carefully setting his ubiquitous pipe on the table. "Is he okay?"

"Damon was the victim of a prank," said Francisco angrily. "Someone slipped some anti-anxiety meds into his drink before the reading. That's the working theory, anyway."

Gasps broke out among the faculty members.

"I still can't fathom how someone could do such a thing," said Calista.

"Unimaginable," agreed Nate.

"How could that have happened? Was he alone before the reading?" Calista asked.

"Not sure," said Francisco. "Was anyone back there with him? I couldn't get my car started and barely made it to the reading on time."

We all affirmed that we were not with Damon.

I thought back to the span of time before the reading. Jasper had said Damon was backstage with Mina, Jasper, and Tally, none of whom would have done it. And I was fairly certain we could also rule out the chancellor as well. He wouldn't have sabotaged his own event when there was money to be solicited.

"Campus Security suggested that perhaps one of the students working at Silver's recognized Damon and spiked his to-go cup," Francisco said. "Or maybe he didn't even know who Damon was and did it for kicks."

There was a long silence, then Spencer took a deep breath and put his hands gently on the table. "Well. That is extremely disturbing. We will have to do our best to make sure the rest of the events go as smoothly as possible."

Everyone nodded dutifully.

Francisco told us Damon had been released from the hospital and was resting. "He's still going to try to make it to the reception tonight."

"Thank you," Spencer said, "for staying on top of the situation."

Calista added her thanks as well. I was glad Francisco was getting some confirmation for his efforts.

"We are also most grateful to Lila for getting Damon here in the first place," Spencer added smoothly, which was kind of him. "And," he continued, "Simone has also done a wonderful job of helping out by getting the students involved."

Members of the faculty looked over and smiled at Simone in her cornflower blue cashmere sweater set and pearls. All Simone had done, as far as I could tell, was blame me for not doing what she'd said *she* would do. I didn't buy her sweet-as-pie routine for one second. But I would let the people of Stonedale discover what lurked beneath that elegant façade on their own. They wouldn't believe me, anyway, if I told them what machinations she was capable of. I could hardly believe it myself.

Calista caught my eye and raised her eyebrows a fraction of an inch. She knew.

"We need to go over the final contracts for the vendors," Spencer continued, motioning to Glynnis, who was standing to my right. She handed me the stack of stapled handout sets, and I passed them along after taking the one on the top. We all sat politely until the papers made their way around the table, though I'm sure a fair majority of individuals had to work to suppress groans at the sight of those thick packets. I had hoped to be able to give my place one last going-over before my mother arrived, but it didn't look likely.

One hour later, we had completed the project with a minimum

of disagreement. We moved on to the new arrangements for Friday night and finalized those details as well. When people began to pack up their materials, I threw my notepad and pen into my bag, then made a run for it.

My key was in the front door lock when I heard a ruckus from the street. A yellow cab screeched to a stop, with my mother, in huge black sunglasses, waving enthusiastically from the back window.

"Lila!" she screamed, as if I wasn't already staring at her.

"Hi Mom." I walked down the sidewalk toward her.

"Hello, darling," she chirped, hopping nimbly out of the cab, despite the stacked heels she'd paired with bright red capri pants. The filmy scarf she'd worn over the red hair cascading down her back added to overall "starlet" impression. Which was of course what she was going for. She tended to dress in character based on her current state of mind. Apparently, this weekend was all about evoking California glamour, even though we were a few states east of that.

She threw her arms around me and gave me a long hug with an extra squeeze for good measure, followed by several hearty smacks on my cheek and a quick survey from head to toe. "You look divine," she pronounced. "Oh, I've missed you."

Her gardenia perfume surrounded me as we waited for the driver to remove two large suitcases from the trunk and place them carefully on the sidewalk. "I brought a few different outfits," she explained, at my look of surprise. "I didn't know what we would be doing."

"Come inside and I'll tell you what's going on," I said, pulling up the handle of one of the suitcases and rolling it behind me.

When we had lugged the suitcases through the front door, she made an appreciative sound. "This is adorable, darling."

"Thanks." I was sure she was shocked at how small the bungalow actually was: just the one small front room with an indentation that served as a dining nook, a galley kitchen at the end, and two bedrooms in the back. The whole thing would have fit into a corner of the first floor of her brownstone, easy.

"And where is your bedroom?"

I led her to the other side of the room into a miniscule hallway, barely large enough to turn around in, with three doors. "That's my bedroom on the left, the office in the middle, and the bathroom on the right."

She praised everything effusively. Moms could be nice like that. "How long is the lease?"

"Just a year, but I have the option to renew. The landlord is one of my neighbors, and she said I can have it as long as I want it."

"I approve. Very cozy."

"It's perfect for one person," I agreed. "And the landlord is great. Sometimes she brings me cookies."

My mother laughed. "While we're on the subject of cookies, do you happen to have any? And perhaps some tea?"

"Wouldn't you rather have lunch to hold you over until the reception?"

She pshawed the idea. My mother had never been what you'd call a regular eater. She often preferred to graze throughout the day with one particularly snacky repast in there somewhere.

I made some peppermint tea and set out Mint Milanos, her favorites, which I'd bought especially for her visit. Thus fortified mint-wise, we settled down at the oak table in my dining nook.

"Happy Valentine's Day, darling," she said. She slid a small box across the table.

"You didn't have to get me anything."

"Yes, I did," she said. "Open it."

I ripped off the wrapping paper and opened the box to find a silver tonneau watch with Roman numerals nestled on a pillow within. Although her gifts had a tendency to demonstrate more of her style than mine, this one was completely on point.

"I love it."

"Here," she said, "let me fasten it for you."

As if I were five. But I obediently held out my arm and let her slide the watch on carefully, then close the clasp. She patted my arm when she finished.

"Thank you so much. It's beautiful." I turned my wrist this way and that several times, admiring it, then hugged her. "I sent your gift to New York because I didn't know you were coming out here."

"How wonderful it will be to have a gift waiting for me when I go home. And I love it already, whatever it is, because it came from you."

We smiled at each other.

"Have you heard from Damon?" I asked. "Does he know you're here?"

"No," she said, brightening. "Won't it be fun to see his face?"

"Mom," I said, "he's probably still recovering. I don't know if he's up for a surprise."

"What do you mean? Did he go on a bender?" Her forehead creased with concern.

"Oh, I didn't tell you yet. He was drugged, apparently."

Her lips formed a perfect "O," and she blinked a few times as she processed the information.

"How in the world did that happen?"

"No one knows, exactly." I filled her in on what Francisco had speculated.

"What was the drug? Where did it come from?"

"Benzodiazepine. Anti-anxiety meds. You'd be surprised at what floats around readily available on college campuses."

"Everyone and their cat seem to be on meds these days. And you know, darling, you can get just about anything on the internet too," she said.

"Good points."

"But, oh, poor Damon." My mother stood up and rooted around in the red leather crossbody bag she'd chosen to match the capris and yanked out her cell phone. Scrolling down to his number, she pressed the send button and shoved the phone up to her ear. She paced back and forth quickly, her face flushing so quickly that I grew concerned.

"Do you feel well, Mom?"

She motioned for me to stop talking—one of those quick, dismissive waves. She could be abrupt when she was concentrating on something, and it was never intended to be hurtful, but it wasn't my favorite thing about her.

After a minute, she hit the off button and sat back down. She took a sip of tea and shifted gears into plan formulation. I had seen her go into that stage so many times before that I had no doubt what was happening.

She sat up straight. "You know where he's staying, right, darling? Let's go over there. I cannot stand this one more minute. He needs to know I'm here to help if he wants me."

"We only have a few hours until we have to leave for the reception. He's probably sleeping, anyway. Why don't you just leave him a voicemail, Mom? Then he can call you back when he's ready."

"That's not how we communicate," she said. Enigmatic perhaps but par for the Violet O course. She just did things her own way, explanations be damned.

As we pulled up to the Mountain Inn, I couldn't shake the sense that this was a mistake. Mom insisted on having her window down to "enjoy the mountain air," so I shivered the whole way there in my wool coat. My mother, however—even with no jacket and her California Girl Capri Look going on—kept saying, "Isn't this invigorating?" She was in her glory, I realized, looking over at her sitting in the passenger's side, with her face offered up to the sunshine, her cheeks aglow. Although drama tended to drain the emotional reserves of most people, it gave her an abundance of energy. Probably one of the character traits that made her such a productive artist: she was able to channel disruptions into creative momentum.

I touched her shoulder gently. She opened her green eyes—I'd inherited the same shade—and swiveled her head to get her bearings, then jumped out of the car as if on springs. I needed to ask her how she managed to be so energetic at all times. I tended to feel more like one of those lumbering bears in Yellowstone who backs up slowly and growls about it the whole way.

"I'll wait for you down—" But she was already gone.

I pulled forward into one of the handy parking spots, locked the car, and went to sit in the warm lobby. Perching on the southwestern sofa next to the chipped table I'd seen before, I checked my phone. There was one text from Calista asking when and where the detective and I would meet them, with a postscript apology for not having followed up with me earlier. That was weird—hadn't she called this morning? I pulled up my recent call list, which showed the last incoming was not Calista but one Lex Archer.

The person I'd thought was my cousin, when I barked out "Can't talk" and clicked off in panic mode due to domestic mayhem, was actually my potential date for the chancellor's reception. And instead of having a civilized conversation like a normal person, I'd hung up on him.

Oops.

Chapter 17

I went into full-on backtracking mode. First, I called Calista and explained what I'd done, begging her to decide where to meet tonight since I could barely think straight, what with my mother in town and the inadvertent pre-first-date rejection of my potential future boyfriend before we'd even had a chance to make arrangements for said initial date. She made some consoling sounds, then some cheerleading noises, then hung up.

I took a deep breath. Needed to be calm, cool, and collected.

I brought up the incoming log again and used the call back function. It rang a few times, but Lex didn't pick up, so I left a voicemail saying I just wanted him to know, if he were interested, that there were plans being made for tonight. We would be meeting inside the party at the chancellor's mansion and he was welcome to come. Not that I meant it as a date or anything but people were going to the reception. The same one we'd mentioned when we ran into each other last night. By mistake. Or on purpose. Or whatever that was. Also, I was sorry for the phone call thing this morning, but I thought it was Calista. Not that I usually did that to her either. In fact, that was the only time I'd *ever* done it. To anyone. In my whole life. Anyway, hoped to see him tonight. Francisco had added his name to the guest list. So he just needed to give his name to the door people. Or the security guards. Or the valets. Really, whoever was working and had a clipboard. At eight. At the chancellor's mansion. As my date or not. Either way.

I yanked the phone away from my mouth in dismay and stared at it, then clicked off before I said anything else.

My mother rushed up to the sofa, red curls waving wildly around her lovely face. "Damon's not up there. I don't know where he is. Can we go to the hospital?"

"No," I said firmly, surprising myself. "We don't even know he's at the hospital. He may just be sleeping. Right now, we're going home."

She took a closer look at my face and nodded. As I drove, she listened very sweetly to me relive the awkwardness that was the voicemail message which had been intended originally to correct the morning's embarrassment but instead had only magnified the humiliation. By the time we got home, I felt better—largely due to her recounting several stories about her own dating mishaps.

The next hour was spent "primping," as my mother called it, and "dressing," as I called it, for the reception. Primping led to a burgundy cocktail gown with glittering jewelry and Jimmy Choos. Dressing led to flowing pants beneath a gothic-flavored black velvet jacket and my favorite boots. Her red curls tumbled prettily down her back; my dark locks were parted in the middle and hung below my shoulders. She was Venus to my Wednesday Addams, as usual.

The chancellor's mansion was a thing of beauty—vast, columned, and spotlighted. It was located west of campus in a gated community. The estate itself had another wrought-iron fence around it for good measure, and we proceeded up the driveway only after our names were checked against the official list at the guardhouse. We pulled up to the portico, and the valet to whom my mother handed the keys gave her a double take. He didn't think I saw him shake then bite his hand in the wake of her va-va-voomness. Good thing she didn't. She would have turned around and given him a lecture on the objectification of women on the spot.

My mother and I walked through the massive double doors into the majestic foyer with a long curving staircase and fountain featuring a statue of some gracefully posed mythological goddess. Our coats were taken by red-vested attendants while we gaped at the magnificence.

I'd never been here before, so I wasn't sure what to expect; we were led through a hallway into a great room with a polished black onyx bar along the left side. The entire back wall was made of windows—I guessed we'd be looking at a spectacular view of the mountains if it weren't dark outside. As it was, the windows overlooked a patio dotted with trees in large planters, festooned with twinkle lights.

Tad appeared, accompanied by a tall blond man—both wearing tuxedos. They were a handsome pair. We made introductions all around. Tad's date was a new Political Science professor from Finland who knew of my mother's work, so I let them chat for a few minutes while I scanned the room for Lex.

Eventually, I caught sight of Calista and Francisco at the bar, and I grabbed my mother's wrist and pulled her gently in that direction. With a great deal of maneuvering and many apologies, we slowly made our way through the numerous crowd members, who were loose from cocktails and gabbing loudly around us. Finally we reached the right side of the onyx bar and greeted the couple. Francisco gave us a jaunty wave and returned to his drink. But Calista swooped in like a hawk who has just spotted her prey.

"Aunt Vi!" she screamed over the din. She gave my mother a fierce hug.

"Hello, my darling." My mother smiled affectionately at Calista, who was lovely in an indigo sheath with an intricate embroidered pattern around the neck. "So happy to see you. How are you?" She gave Calista another hug.

"Just fine," my cousin said. "Better now that you're here, Aunt Vi. Can't wait to catch up. Can I get you both a drink?"

"I'd love a champagne," my mother said. "Lila?"

"The same." I leaned against an open space on the bar, scanning the crowd again for Lex in a manner I hoped was unobtrusive.

"He's not here," Calista said, reaching behind me to accept champagne flutes from the bartender. And here I'd thought I was being so stealthy. "Yet," she added. She reached out and stroked the velvet sleeve of my jacket. "Ooh. Now that's one enticing fabric. Excellent choice. He won't be able to keep his hands off of you."

"Calista!"

She handed me a glass of champagne. "Drink this and relax. He'll either be here or he won't. Try to enjoy the night either way."

Nate, handsome in a black suit with a red tie, walked up and greeted us. He squeezed my shoulder with his left hand while he pulled his waiflike companion in a rose-colored dress around in a swirl until she came to rest in front of me. It put me in mind of twisting a cone of cotton candy. Her dark blue eyes sparkled as she laughed up at him.

"Lila, this is Amanda."

My stomach tightened. I don't know why Nate having a girlfriend bothered me. I didn't want to date him, for goodness sakes. Maybe it was just that I liked having all of his attention to myself. If so, I deserved a stern talking-to.

"Nice to meet you," I said, with a huge smile to counter my thoughts.

"You too," she said in a friendly tone. She gave me what seemed to be a genuinely warm smile, revealing her straight white teeth. Her brown hair was the kind of glossy silk you only see achieved in shampoo commercials, her cheeks a lovely shade of pink, and her lashes so long that they almost touched her perfectly shaped eyebrows. Yet she didn't seem to be wearing any makeup.

I chugged the rest of my champagne.

"I've heard so much about you." She tilted her head toward Nate. "He thinks you're pretty cool."

Nate gave her a tiny shoulder jab. "Hey, you're not supposed to tell her that."

She laughed again, so infectiously I found myself laughing too.

Dang it. I didn't want to *like* her.

Hearing our laughter, Calista and my mother paused in their

animated conversation about Cindy Sherman's art and drew closer.

Nate busied himself getting drinks while everyone had themselves a swift meet-and-greet with his girlfriend.

We learned that she taught literature at Colorado State University, she had already done two Fulbrights—the latest of which was in France—and she ran marathons, which explained her otherworldly slenderness.

My mother pounced on the France thing—Paris being a subject that made her wax rhapsodic—and the two of them drifted around the corner of the bar, deep in conversation. I caught the occasional French phrase interjected into their conversation and knew Amanda was going to be well occupied for the next few minutes.

"Did you hear about Damon?" I asked Nate.

"Francisco told me," he said, his eyes wide. "That's insane."

"Were you at the reading? I didn't see you there."

"No. On the way home from class, Amanda found a hurt dog on the sidewalk. Someone had hit it with a car and kept going, can you believe it?" Disgust crossed his face. "Anyway, she raced it to the vet. She has such a good heart." He looked proudly over at Amanda chattering away with my mother. "I was waiting for her, and she didn't get down to Stonedale until very late, so we missed it."

"Well, it's great she could be here for Valentine's Day."

"I know, right? Perfect timing."

"She seems nice." I meant it, unfortunately.

"She is," he said, his expression verging on lovestruck at the thought of her.

So far, my plan to not care about Nate's girlfriend was not working very well.

Soon afterwards, we were urged by wandering red-vested individuals to return to the grand foyer. Caught in the slow shuffle of guests making their way toward the front of the house, I looked around for Lex once again, hoping the throng would shift and there he would be: leaning against the wall, looking suave in some kind of noir-esque suit. Maybe eyeing everyone suspiciously because that's what detectives did. Or maybe he'd be smiling pleasantly since he was off-duty. Or maybe he would be scowling, annoyed that I'd invited him in such a rambling way, then never actually found him.

At last we moved into the foyer, where the chancellor stood on the small landing at the bottom of the staircase, facing the guests. The two steps down between him and the crowd were, of course, intentional.

"Good evening," Chancellor Wellington said heartily. "Thanks so much for joining us tonight to celebrate one of the twentieth century's...er..." He faltered for a moment, evidently checking the calendar in his head. "Twenty-*first* century's greatest writers, Damon Von Tussel."

Everyone applauded.

The chancellor held his palms out and made a patting motion to indicate that we should stop.

"Patsy and I welcome you." He glanced at the blue-gowned and inexplicably tiara-ed Mrs. Wellington, who was positioned to the chancellor's left, but one step down, facing the crowd as well. She gave a royal wave—the vague kind with minimal wrist movement which says "you're not worth expending energy for"— and smiled back up at him. "Mr. Von Tussel will be joining us in a short while. In the meantime, please enjoy a libation and an *amuse-bouche*. The Stonedale University String Quartet will be serenading you with a collection of songs selected specifically for this special holiday—we wish a very happy Valentine's to all."

As the sweet strains of "Some Enchanted Evening" floated into the air, the crowd began to break apart and redistribute themselves between the foyer and the large room with the bar we'd just come from. I paused at the edge of the fountain and surveyed the room, catching sight of Calista and Francisco going through the doorway to the great room, followed by Nate and Amanda. I craned my neck seeking my mother, but she seemed to have disappeared.

The babbling sounds of the fountain muted the string quartet somewhat, but it didn't bother me. In fact, I was not really in the mood for romantic songs. Everyone seemed to be part of a couple right now—except me. That hadn't been an issue for me before, but for some reason, I felt it keenly tonight. Maybe it was the excess of love symbols strewn across Stonedale for Valentine's Day. You couldn't go ten feet without bumping into a paper heart taped onto something. I was staring down into the water of the fountain, giving over to the melancholy saturating my state of mind, when someone called my name.

Mina and Jasper stood before me, holding hands. Her hair was pinned up in a complicated style, and she wore a black corset over a long cinnamon shift. The effect was rather Renaissance Fair but it looked charming on her. Jasper was slightly more subdued in a black suit, but the collar of his red shirt was embossed in the hipster style. They really made the perfect couple, sartorially. I wonder if they'd planned it.

"Have you seen my father?" Mina asked. She darted glances around the room. "He's supposed to be mingling, but we can't find him."

"We will," Jasper said comfortingly.

"No, I haven't seen him," I said. "Would you like me to help you look for him?" Something to do would be nice, actually. I was sort of sick of myself at the moment.

"Would you?" Mina said, her shoulders visibly relaxing. "We looked all over the first floor already. Let's go upstairs."

"How is he?" I asked as we walked toward the staircase. I wasn't sure we should be going to the second floor. Typically, parties at places like this were meant to take place on the lower level. I hoped we didn't run into the chancellor. Or even Patsy.

Jasper led the way as Mina ascended beside me.

"He's a little weak," she confided.

"He's fine," Jasper shot over his shoulder.

She made a face at Jasper's back going around the curve in the stairs.

"I didn't think my father should come tonight, but he insisted."

"Do you know what happened?"

Her lips tight, she shook her head. "Just that someone drugged him."

"That's horrible," I said.

"Disgusting," she agreed angrily.

We took the remaining steps in silence. At the top, all three of us paused for a second and scanned the long hallway. There were about twenty closed doors. We had our work cut out for us.

As we began checking rooms down the first side, we passed numerous niches holding white busts in the classical style. I stepped over to one of them, a woman with a graceful curved neck, and saw a copper plate beneath engraved with the name "Juno." The next one had a more jaunty pose, her head up, alert, as if addressing something head on. Her label said "Minerva." So these were Roman goddesses.

Mina slid up next to me. "That's my mother's name."

"Wonderful name. Is it yours too?"

"Yes, though no one has ever called me anything but Mina." She smiled, as if remembering something fondly. "You know, my mother hated the name at first...thought it was far too grand for a girl from Brooklyn."

"That was her real name? I thought she'd chosen it when she became a model," I said. "Because she was so tall and fierce."

"It was real. Minerva Babylonia Clark." She laughed. "My grandmother was Italian, and my grandfather, who was English, pretty much let her have her way with everything. So that's what she picked. Eventually my mother came to appreciate the name— she found it had a sort of strength—and gave it to me." She trailed her hand gently over the engraved letters on the copper nameplate. "They're all gone now though."

"I'm sorry." I still felt horrible for asking Mina about her mother when we first met. I didn't want to say the wrong thing now, so I wandered away, leaving her to her thoughts.

We continued checking rooms separately. Near the end of the hallway, I saw a narrow elevator and whistled. Mina came over.

"Wow," she said. "That's handy."

I agreed and pushed the call button.

Her eyebrows rose.

"Just want to give it a try," I said. The doors opened noiselessly to reveal a closet-sized space with damask wallpaper in shades of beige and bronze.

"Fancy," she murmured.

The sound of a door opening startled me. Jasper had gone into a nearby room. Mina and I hurried over to join him. It was full of some truly exquisite furniture and tapestries, the kind an interior designer has to have imported.

"Nothing here," Jasper said.

"Except magnificence," Mina said. "It's incredible."

"I agree," I said. I couldn't even fathom having something this luxurious to come home to. Although this was probably just a guest room for the Wellingtons. My mother's brownstone in New York was very nice by most people's standards, but this place was on a whole different level.

As we worked our way down the opposite side back toward the staircase, we heard a thump in one of the remaining rooms.

The three of us froze and stared at each other.

There was another thump.

"What the—" Mina ran to the vicinity of the sound and threw open the door.

And there was her father. With my mother. Becoming reacquainted.

Chapter 18

Mina yelped and slammed the door shut again.

"Were they..." I couldn't bring myself to end the sentence.

"No, no. Thank God. No." She closed her eyes. "Just kissing."

Whew.

After a long minute, the door opened and my mother came out, squinting in the well-lit hallway. Her clothes were disheveled, and she pushed her hair back into place with both hands and gave me a sheepish smile. I did not smile back. I was so embarrassed I could not have spoken if I wanted to.

"Hi Violet," said Mina.

"Hi Mina," my mother said, giving us both a hug.

Damon stepped through the doorway, straightening his tie. His cane was hooked over his lower wrist. "Need something?" It came out brusquely.

Mina sighed. "You're wanted downstairs. To mingle."

He rolled his eyes but headed toward the staircase without complaint. We followed the Parade of Shame down the stairs, through the foyer, past the fountain, and into the great room.

Damon was instantly surrounded by people eager to meet him. Mina and Jasper took up a position on either side of him, perhaps to protect him, but it looked like a family portrait. Which I guess was fitting since, after the wedding, they'd be family officially.

My mother whispered into my ear, "I'm sorry, darling. I'd forgotten how charming he could be—"

Charming? Were we talking about the same man?

"—and before I knew it, we were in each other's arms. Maybe it was the romantic music or the champagne. We were just swept away."

I put my hand up to prevent hearing any more. "Please stop, Mother."

She chuckled and patted my cheek. "You need to loosen up, darling. Let me get you another glass of champagne."

I watched her drift gracefully through the crowd, then wheeled around to get myself some fresh air.

The chilly air out front soothed my overheated skin. I stood next to a large coach light and tried to calm down. My mother had always done outrageous things; that was part of her modus operandi as an artist. If there was a rule, my mother was going to break it. A line, she'd step over it. It had been very difficult to rebel when I was a teenager because she herself was all about rebellion.

She practically cheered the one and only time I got in trouble in high school. And the sad thing was, it hadn't even been true. Someone had misidentified me as the person responsible for scrawling a swear word on the bathroom wall. It made my mother so happy to hear I had finally "broken out of my shell"—as she called it—that I didn't tell her the truth. Most kids were lying about what they had done; I couldn't admit what I hadn't.

Sometimes it felt like I was the mother and she was the child.

Yet nothing had prepared me for the day my mother would make out with her ex-boyfriend in the upstairs bedroom of the chancellor of my university's home.

We were definitely going to have to talk about that.

I walked back into the foyer, determined to greet my department colleagues, then make a run for it. It should be clear I had done what was expected, attend the event, but I wanted to go home. The combination of the enforced romantic environment of Valentine's Day and the actual couples surrounding me everywhere I looked created an overwhelming desire to flee. Plus, there was the humiliation of not being able to stop hoping I'd see Lex coming to meet me. Not to mention my mother and Damon's disconcerting reunion. Yes, it was time to go.

For the second time that evening, I found myself standing next to the fountain, unwilling to join the crowd in the other room. I noticed a few familiar faces—Tad and his adorable date, Willa, and Jasper—making their way through the titanic front doors toward the valets. Maybe I could also get away without making another round through the crowd. As I pondered the benefits of either choice, Damon came through the doorway from the great room and headed directly for the staircase. I hoped he and my mother weren't planning to go for another round. I glanced up to see if she was waiting for him there and caught sight of something hurtling through the air.

I raced over and pushed Damon against the wall as hard as I could.

"Hey!" he protested as he flew through the air, his cane clattering noisily on the ground.

Then the object crashed down on the marble floor behind me, the loud sound ricocheting off of the walls as white pieces exploded around us. After a moment, we both unfroze and peered at the fragments.

"It's one of the busts from upstairs," I murmured.

"What the hell was *that*?" Damon bellowed. "What's wrong with this place? Can't a man move an inch without being accosted in one way or another?

"I'm sorry," I said. "I saw it falling and had to push you out of the way."

"I don't mean you," Damon said, perhaps one degree less belligerently. "I mean that." He gestured to the fragments scattered over a large portion of the foyer.

We both looked up. No one was there. Obviously.

People came running from the other room and surrounded us. Damon was waving his arms and trying to keep anyone from touching him. I was answering the questions peppered at me from all angles and simultaneously asking Damon to please stop smacking everyone. It was chaos.

After a few minutes, my mother and Mina pushed their way to the front of the crowd. I was relieved to leave them to it.

"Are you okay?" I asked. "Can I get you anything?"

"A whiskey," he said. "Double."

I nodded and began to walk away.

He grabbed my left arm, holding me back. "Thanks," he said gruffly. "Good reflexes."

Feeling oddly uplifted by his words—or maybe it was the adrenaline racing through my veins—I made my way through the group of onlookers who had gathered in the foyer. As I journeyed back to the bar once again, I said hello to several colleagues as well as the chancellor. Mission accomplished, workwise.

And then I ran into Lex. Leaning against the bar, chatting with Calista and Francisco, looking every bit as suave as I had imagined he would. Right before I reached him, he laughed, looking surprisingly at ease for once. Also handsome. I strode up and said hello.

Coolly.

He could have called me back, after all.

Turning my back on Lex, I ordered Damon's whiskey from the young bartender and drummed my fingers on the onyx while I waited, the picture of nonchalance. Or so I hoped.

Lex tapped me on the shoulder. I spun around.

"Yes?"

"I was looking for you."

"Oh?" I inwardly applauded my blasé tone.

"Yes. Quite hard, actually."

"Well, I've been here all night. You must not be a very good detective."

"Darn it." He grinned.

I smiled despite myself, then remembered we had a situation and snapped my fingers. "Actually, we need a professional right now. Someone almost hit Damon Von Tussel with a statue."

He blinked twice quickly. "Are you joking?"

"Not at all. Come with me." I grabbed the drink the bartender had produced and motioned for Lex to follow me. As we walked, I told him what had just happened. He clenched his jaw and lowered his eyelids, as if he were shifting from party mode to detective mode. When we came around the corner, he pulled out his badge and held it up.

"Excuse me—police business. Please clear the area." The crowd parted quickly, and he knelt next to Damon, who was now sitting on the ground leaning against the wall. My mother was on one side with her arm around him, patting his shoulder. Mina was on the other, speaking intently to him, and Jasper was next to her, doing something on his phone. I thrust the drink at Damon while Lex asked him to recount what had happened. Damon's version was basically the same as mine, though he opened with "I was just walking along, minding my own business, when Lila came *charging* at me..."

No good deed goes unpunished, apparently.

It wasn't much of a crime scene, just a broken statue, but Lex explored it like the pro that he was. He even snapped some shots of the fragment pattern on the floor, and the area directly above, and the empty alcove where the bust of Minerva had once stood. I didn't know if he was going to file an official report or if this was just habit for him, but it was nice to know someone had examined the evidence.

"Why did it have to be Minerva?" Mina looked sad. "I wouldn't have minded if Juno had been broken. But Minerva reminded me of my mother."

Jasper gave her a quick hug. "We should get one for our place. When we're married."

She smiled at the thought. "I would love one. So I guess something good came out of this."

Lex returned and informed us that he was done.

"Unless you can think of anything else?"

We all shook our heads.

"Please call me if you have any information." He made a trip around the circle, handing out business cards, then everyone drifted slowly away.

"Well, Lila," he said, "you certainly live a dangerous life. Aside from the café, it seems like most times I see you, someone has just been attacked in one way or another. What is it about you?" He cocked his head, studying me.

"That's not fair," I protested.

"Really? Name one exception."

I wracked my brain, then smiled triumphantly. "Nothing happened at Roland's memorial service last year."

"What about to Roland?"

"But that was *before* the service started."

Lex considered this. "Fine. I'll let you have that one." He moved closer and peered into my face, speaking quietly. "But seriously, are you okay?"

I took a deep breath and checked in with myself. "I was moving before I knew what I was doing, so there wasn't really any time to be scared."

"That was brave." He rubbed my arm slowly, which sent minor tremors down my spine.

"The adrenaline is wearing off, I think," I said. He inched slightly closer. The air between us was charged with tension, and I wasn't sure how I felt about that.

I didn't dislike it though.

"Lila!" Nate was suddenly at my elbow, the lovely Amanda in tow. I took a step back from the detective and was surprised to see a flash of irritation cross his face at being interrupted.

Nate and Amanda wanted to hear about the accident. Lex walked away and took a call on his cell phone while we chatted. A few minutes later, he mouthed, "I have to go." I excused myself from the audience of two, promising to return momentarily.

"Work," Lex said, gesturing with his phone. "Walk me out?"

We crossed the foyer and went out the front door. Most of the party guests had left, so the front drive was empty except for a lone red-vested valet leaning against the wall who stood up at our approach; he looked somewhat hopeful, perhaps anticipating a tip. Lex gave him the paper ticket, and he scuttled away toward wherever Lex's car was parked.

"Look," he said. "This night didn't really turn out the way I'd hoped. May I take you to dinner on Friday?"

He'd hoped for something? I bookmarked that for future consideration.

"Damon's reading is on Friday."

"Oh right, they rescheduled it." He stared across the front drive for a long minute. "Are you going?"

"Yes," I said. "Mandatory. Even if my mother weren't suddenly attached to his right arm, I'd have to go for work."

"Ah."

"I'd ask you to accompany me, but it's probably not your thing."

"What, pray tell, do you think my *thing* is?"

I pondered that for a moment. His white smile was very bright and kind of distracting. "Something with explosions?" I ventured finally.

He rolled his eyes.

"Car chases?"

"Talk about stereotypes," he scoffed. "C'mon Professor. Stretch."

"Then you tell me. One of your things."

He chuckled but said nothing.

"You're going to make me work for this, aren't you?"

He waited.

"I give up."

Still didn't move a muscle.

I sighed. "Okay, you enjoy..." I inspected him from head to toe. "Training bonsai trees."

His mouth fell open. "Where did *that* come from?"

"I don't know," I confessed. "It was the furthest thing from explosions I could think of."

He laughed, a deep sound surprising me with its richness and warmth. It was the kind of laugh that made you want to laugh along. So I did.

"What's so funny?" Nate said from the doorway. I smiled at him but didn't explain.

Amanda echoed the question. I ignored her too.

Lex squeezed my arm and started toward his car, which the valet just pulled up to the curb. "I'll call you about dinner," he said over his shoulder.

Last time his calling me had led to my hanging up on him, followed by the disastrous voicemail message.

But at least he was willing to try again. That was a positive sign.

I watched him walk away, moving in his trademark style, which always reminded me of a secret service guy—all virile and powerful energy coiled up beneath a bland exterior. But then I remembered the way he had looked when he laughed tonight and upgraded "bland" to "appealing."

"Good night, Detective," said Nate, appearing at my elbow for the second time that night, Amanda trailing again behind him like a small cloud. She was so ethereal she just seemed to float everywhere.

He smiled down at me. I felt oddly irritated with him. It was fine he was with Amanda, but he didn't have to keep bringing her over to me.

"So, did he meet you here or..." Nate trailed off.

"Yes," I said. I was glad he'd worded it that way rather than asking me if we were on a date. I wasn't even sure myself if we had actually been on a date or if Lex had showed up thinking it was a group thing. Or maybe his crime-fighter sense had tingled and he had come here to take care of business.

But we were going out to dinner, in any case. That was definitely a date.

"Wherever did you meet him?" asked Amanda, looking extremely interested. "He's yummy."

Lex gave me a wave and drove away slowly and carefully. I liked that he didn't have to peel out to show what a man he was, like some of my ex-boyfriends who seemed to believe women liked the squeal of tires.

Amanda interrupted my thoughts with a soft touch on my forearm. "Really, where did you meet him?"

"Oh, he thought I committed a murder," I said airily.

Her double take was priceless.

Chapter 19

I stood under the portico waiting for a valet to materialize. My mother had decided to go with Damon to his hotel to keep an eye on him, but I didn't mind having a moment alone. There was only so much crowd I could handle, and the Arts Week events had exhausted me. I closed my eyes and concentrated on letting go of the tension in my shoulders. The cold air was refreshing, even though it made me shiver.

My tiny serenity bubble was popped when Mina rushed up and seized my arm, her face pale. "Someone pushed me down the stairs," she said in a shaky voice.

"When? Are you okay?"

"Just now." She grabbed my other forearm and clutched them both as if she were a drowning person and I was the lifeguard.

"Okay, take a deep breath and let it out slowly."

She did as I said, and we went through it several more times until her trembling lessened.

"Better?"

She nodded. "Thank you."

"Are you hurt?"

"Dazed mostly. I'll have some bruises, for sure, but I don't think I broke anything."

"That's good," I said. "What happened? Can you walk me through it?"

She let go of me and wrapped her arms around herself instead.

"I went inside to get my purse...I think I dropped it when we saw your mom and my dad...you know."

We both made a face at the thought.

"They've been turning lights off inside, and the upstairs hallway was dark. It freaked me out, so I ran over, grabbed my purse and returned to the staircase quickly. When I was right at the top, I heard a door close. I started to turn around, but before I could see who was behind me, I was falling."

"Did you look back up the staircase after you fell?"

"Of course. But no one was there."

It would have been so much easier if the culprit had just stuck around.

"We should tell someone."

She shook her head emphatically. "I don't want to worry my father. He's already poised to leave town as it is."

"I think we should tell him."

"Lila, please don't. I'm fine. Really." She moved her neck slowly from side to side, stretching—or checking—it. "If you tell him, you won't have a reader on Friday."

"If you're hurt, that's more important. Could we at least go to urgent care, get you checked out? I can drive you."

"No," she said, seeming steadier now. "Jasper will be here soon."

"Where are they? Didn't you come together?"

"Yes, but they went to get the car. Jasper didn't want the valet to drive the rental. He didn't buy the insurance, so now he's obsessing over every potential scratch that could happen." She laughed.

A laugh was a good sign, right?

"I would have bought the insurance and let the scratches fall where they may," she added.

"Me too," I said. "Do you want me to walk you to the car?"

"No—here they are," she said, pointing to the shiny black SUV pulling up to the curb. Jasper, who was driving, made a hurry-up motion. Damon stared out the window from the passenger seat as the door on the side of the car slid back automatically. My mother waved gaily at me from the backseat. I waved back.

"Have a good night," I called out.

Mina walked a few steps toward the car, then doubled back to give me a hug. "Thanks for helping me."

"I'm glad you're okay," I said.

"Remember, not a word of this to anyone, okay?" Her eyes were locked on mine.

"Okay," I said. "But if it can help us figure out who is behind all of this, I might have to mention it to Detective Archer."

She shrugged. "Fair enough. But no one else."

"Deal."

The rest of the week flew by as I taught classes, did some advising, and tried to catch up on my grading. My mother, who appeared to have appointed herself official bodyguard, spent most of the week with Damon, Mina, and Jasper. Although I knew it wouldn't have been fun for her to sit around my empty house while I was at campus, I did worry about her being in such close proximity to the trio who had been targeted by persons unknown. I couldn't convince her to stay away; in fact, she tried to urge me to spend even more time with them. On Thursday night, under my mother's orders, I showed up at The Peak House, where we were meeting Damon, Jasper, and Mina for dinner.

"Darling!" My mother, in a chic black suit and pumps, came forward to greet me. "We're sitting over here." She led the way through the full restaurant to the booth where I'd seen Simone's mother last time. I paused for a moment to imagine the two maternal forces meeting.

Pretty sure my mom could take her mom.

We arrived at the wooden table where Damon, Jasper, and Mina were already having cocktails. The three of them were on one side of the long table, with Mina in the middle. I sat next to my mother on the other side and greeted the group.

We chatted for awhile about the places they'd gone this week.

"Garden of the Gods was beautiful, but I could hardly breathe at the top of Pikes Peak," said Mina. "I mean, I walked two feet and almost fainted. Luckily, Jasper caught me." She smiled at him fondly.

He put his arm around her shoulders, pulling her closer.

"And the drive down—all twists and turns."

She shuddered.

"We made it," Jasper said, running his free hand through his spiky hair. "No worries."

"Builds character," Damon boomed. "Man versus nature."

"Or car versus car," Mina said, elbowing him.

"That too," Damon said, winking at her before taking a slug of his whiskey.

"What's the plan for tomorrow?" he asked Jasper.

Jasper straightened up instantly and removed his arm from Mina's shoulder in order to lean forward and face Damon. "The whole day is free until the reading."

"Is there anything you'd like to do?" I asked Damon.

"Get out of this one-horse town," he snapped.

Nice attitude. We'd paid him double his usual rate for the displeasure of his company. The least he could do was be polite about it. I refrained from comment.

"The sooner we get back to New York, the better." Damon slapped the table for emphasis, which startled me. He saw me jump and gave a phlegmy chortle, studying me from underneath furrowed brows, the thick white hairs clumped like two furry caterpillars holding on for dear life. Eventually, he turned to Jasper. "I don't want to do anything tomorrow but sleep late, eat some good food, and get this whole thing over with. Where in tarnation is our waiter, by the way?"

"I'll go find him," Jasper offered, leaping up from the table.

"Would you like to go for a walk?" my mother asked Damon. "Might be nice to stretch our legs before dinner."

"No," he said, crossing his arms over his chest like a stubborn toddler. He probably knew he was going to get an earful for snapping at me.

"Oh, let's stroll a little," she said, going over to him and rubbing his arm. "It's lovely outside."

He sighed loudly and made a big production of standing up as slowly as possible.

"Order me a steak," he said to Mina. "Rare. Baked potato loaded. Skip the salad."

She nodded.

My mother asked if I wouldn't mind ordering her a California Club salad. She stressed the *please*, maybe to teach Damon some manners.

I could hear him grumbling as he trailed behind her.

Once he'd left, the energy in the room lightened. It was as though someone had opened a window and fresh air had come streaming in.

The server arrived and took our orders, then Mina and I were left looking at each other across the table. She held up her left hand and straightened her engagement ring so that the large diamond was in the middle again.

I complimented her ring.

"Thank you," she said, holding it out so I could do a closer inspection. "It belonged to Jasper's mother. She passed away. His father too. Sailing accident."

"I'm sorry."

"I didn't really know her," she said softly. "Otherwise I would always be sad when I looked at it."

"So how did you and Jasper meet?" I asked her.

"Grad school, though it was because of my father." She looked down for a long moment. "I was at boarding school when my mother and grandparents died—"

"I'm sorry," I said again.

"Thank you," she said flatly. She lifted her chin and her eyes softened. "And I didn't have anyone left in the world besides Damon. He was so good to me when I was young—my mother and I lived next door to him, and we spent as much time in his loft as we did in our own. They were my family, even though I didn't know he was my real father until right before my mother died."

"That's when she told you?"

"Yes. She was going through a deep depression near the end, though none of us knew it was the end, of course. I mean, she might have known. The overdose could have been a suicide." Mina looked down and twisted her ring again. "At boarding school, I missed them both tremendously. Damon doesn't like to talk on the phone or email or write letters, so it was as if he disappeared. After college, I decided to apply to grad schools in New York to be close to him."

"And you were reunited."

"Yes, and it was wonderful." She smiled at me. "Word got out during my first year at school that I was Damon's daughter. So of course Jasper started to pay more attention to me: he was writing his dissertation on my father's work, and he began to ask me questions about his earlier years. I tried to fill in the gaps for him and, in return, he helped me understand the literary significance of my father's work. I'd already spoken to Columbia about housing my father's papers, and I needed to learn as much as possible. Jasper knows everything there is to know about Damon Von Tussel's work and reception. It was like having a crash course designed just for me."

"Are you a doctoral student too?"

"No. I'm in the master's program, creative writing. And you know how complicated literary theory is—you can't just process it like that." She snapped her fingers. "Anyway, Jasper and I spent a lot of time together, and we fell in love."

"Sounds like it was meant to be."

"It was." Her eyes sparkled.

The server delivered a round of drinks. Taking advantage of the fact that most of my dining companions were not available to look at me askance, I relocated a heap of cubes from my water glass into my cabernet.

Mina raised her eyebrows.

"I call it a 'wine slushie.' Apologies if you are a purist."

"Slush away. In fact, I'll give it a try myself." After performing the identical maneuver, she swirled her glass for a moment then tasted it. "I can't believe I've never done that before. I may now be in danger of increasing my wine intake."

"Cheers." I held up my glass. She clinked mine and we both took a sip. Heavenly.

"How are you feeling after your fall down the stairs?"

"I'm fine. A few tender spots, but it scared me more than anything else. I'm embarrassed that I let it rile me up so much."

"It would have riled up anyone," I consoled her. "Any idea about who might have done it?"

She looked around the restaurant before leaning forward and lowering her voice. I leaned forward too. "You know Alonzo and Gilles? They're kind of creepy. I wouldn't put it past them."

"What do you mean by 'creepy'?"

She turned the stem of her wineglass a few times before answering. "They're obsessed with my father. This week, they've been begging Jasper to invite them along wherever Damon is going. It's very trying for Jasper. I mean, he likes them and all, but...enough is enough."

"I thought he'd been good friends with them for awhile."

"They do go to the same conferences," she said. "I don't know how much interaction they have in between. You're right though— he was glad they were going to be on the same panel here. Plus..." She trailed off, looking uncomfortable.

"What?"

"Well, they agreed that participating had the added bonus of proving themselves to Francisco, whom all three have come to fear over the years because Francisco always questions points in their papers at conferences in a really condescending way." She gave me a commiserative look. "And you know how sensitive scholars are."

I acknowledged that with a nod. Even though I was one.

"Have you read Jasper's dissertation?" I asked her.

"I have," she said. "He was pretty adamant about not letting me see it—like all the stressed-out grad students we know who are plagued with self-doubt—but I finally made it happen."

"How?"

She raised an eyebrow. "Honey, we're engaged. I gave him a kiss and picked his pocket."

That should be a bumper sticker.

"Just kidding. I snagged his cell phone when he went out for a run and read the backup copy he emailed to himself. He was furious at first, but then he came to appreciate my enthusiastic commentary. Anyway, I'm the only one who has seen it besides his advisors and the university press publishing it."

A university press publication right away meant Jasper would probably be snapped up by some school very quickly. I wondered if they'd talked about the fact that it might be somewhere far away from NYC. She seemed so intent on being near Damon.

I didn't bring it up. None of my business, anyway.

Jasper returned and performed a quick drum roll on the table top. "You're never going to believe this, babe. My grandmother is coming to Stonedale tomorrow."

Mina looked stunned. "The one from Iowa?"

"The very same," he said, grinning. "I sent her a picture from when we went to Royal Gorge, which led to a discussion about why we were in Colorado, blah blah blah. Anyway, long story short: she wants to meet you."

Mina blushed becomingly and smoothed back her hair.

"She's a character. You'll love her. After the reading, we can all have dinner together."

"I can't wait," she said, beaming at him.

Jasper slid into the booth. "Wait, what were you guys talking about?"

"You," Mina said.

"Good things, I hope."

"Yes, about how brilliant your dissertation is."

He lit up. "You're biased."

"Perhaps," she said sweetly, "But it's still true. Then I was telling Lila about Gilles and Alonzo being kind of pushy..."

Jasper rolled his eyes. "They just keep asking to get to Damon. Then they act all ticked off that I can't make it happen."

"How far do you think they'd go?" I asked. "Could they have anything to do with what's been going on this week? Are they maybe resentful in an if-we-can't-have-Damon-nobody-can kind of way?"

He raised one eyebrow. "Might you be overthinking things?"

"I'm a professor. That's what we do."

He grinned. "Touché."

I kept pressing. "So do you think Gilles and Alonzo may be possible suspects?"

Mina nodded immediately, but Jasper leaned back and considered the question. "I'm not sure," he said slowly. "They were onstage during the panel, right? So how could they be involved?"

"Good point," Mina admitted. "But maybe they got someone else to drop the spotlight."

"Why, though?" Jasper said, looking vaguely sick—perhaps at the memory of being hit.

"They could be jealous of you," I said.

"Yes," Mina added firmly. "They are completely jealous of Jasper."

"But why would they drug Damon?"

We all sat and pondered this.

"I don't understand how criminal minds work," Jasper said finally. "But I do know that the night he was drugged, Damon's cup was just sitting there in the green room, and anyone could have dosed it."

"Right," Mina agreed. "People were coming in and out the whole time. And we walked down the hall to speak to the chancellor—"

"And another time to talk to a reporter—" Jasper interjected.

"Though Damon didn't give him a single quote he could use." Mina laughed.

"As usual," Jasper said, chuckling along with her.

It reminded me of my own attempt to get a quote. Although it had only been a few weeks ago, it seemed like eons. So much had happened since then.

One more event, then this Arts Week nightmare was over. I just hoped we all made it through safely.

Chapter 20

My mother had elected to spend the night with Damon, so when I awoke the next morning, the house was quiet. After taking care of some quotidian duties, I made myself a pot of coffee and settled down on my sofa with the laptop.

I was surprised to discover, at the top of my inbox, an email from my ex-boyfriend Zane, as if he'd known somehow that he—or his bad driving, to be precise—had fleetingly crossed my mind last night so had dutifully responded. We'd had a horrible breakup in grad school, involving cheating (him) and crying (me).

I still remembered the confusion of our final night as a couple—watching him walk out of a party hand in hand with an unfamiliar blonde, even though Zane and I had been together for several years. It turned my stomach even now to think of it. They had paused on the threshold of the house and kissed; her hair was backlit by the porch light, so she looked like some kind of angel. I stared in disbelief, clutching my cup of cheap beer, unable to move or make a sound. Then Zane leaned over to close the door, his longish brown hair brushing against his cheek in the sexy way that had made me fall for him in the first place. He never looked up.

And I had never looked back.

I thought briefly about opening the email to see if he had finally composed a long-overdue apology, which would be healing. Then again...

Delete.

I was grateful that common sense prevailed, which wasn't

usually the case for me. Where Zane was concerned, however, an iron will was in order.

I clicked on the next one without really looking. As soon as I read it, I froze.

Do not let Damon Von Tussel read tonight. This is your final warning.

Again with the anonymous threats? Goosebumps dotted my arms. I didn't know if it was a crackpot or the person who was responsible for the recent attacks. And frankly, I didn't want to know. I checked the header on the email: it had a different email address and sender from the first one, but that didn't mean much. It only takes two seconds to set up a new email account. Even though the whole committee had probably received the same email, I immediately forwarded it to Spencer, the dean, and the chancellor. I knew they were in touch with the authorities and taking precautions as necessary. After a slight hesitation, I forwarded it to Lex as well—we'd already told him about the first email, and I'd rather err on the side of caution in this case.

Although the anonymous threats were alarming, I couldn't allow myself to dwell on them if I was going to make it through the final event of Arts Week. I deliberately turned my attention to the rest of my inbox, trying to ignore the misgivings I felt about tonight, and soon I'd waded through the rest of my emails. Typical fare: notices about university activities, pleas from students for help and/or extensions, and department business. Judith had also emailed to remind me I had promised to facilitate the discussion on Gertrude Stein's *Tender Buttons* at an upcoming meeting of the Stonedale Literary Society. I sketched out a quick outline of ideas. It was one of my favorite Stein texts, so that was a bonus.

Speaking of books, I wished the university press would respond more quickly to my proposal. It had only been a few days since I had clicked submit, and I couldn't stop wondering when I might hear from them, even though I knew not to expect a response for at least several months or more. I fully expected them to reject it, after what Willa had said. But it would be a relief to get it over with so I could move on.

I paused, wondering if I should just write the next proposal for editing Isabella's novels and send it along to be considered with my existing proposal. At least that way, the publisher would know the author about whom I'd written was an existing literary voice.

But no one submitted a book proposal on top of an existing book proposal, right? The press would think I didn't know what I was doing.

I didn't know what I was doing, of course, but I didn't want them to *think* that.

I had faith in my topic, regardless of being new to the submission process. Isabella Dare deserved to be known. And everyone who submitted work had to start somewhere. Perhaps someday—some glorious day in the future—I'd finally be a full professor, with a few books under my belt even. Perhaps Future Full Professor Me would have accomplished enough to satisfy university requirements at last and could thereafter glide across campus without a care in the world.

At the present time, I could not even imagine such a thing. All I felt now was frantic to prepare each class well, frantic to grade and return papers in a reasonable amount of time, frantic to complete the necessary service work, and frantic to publish enough to keep this job. On the positive side, I had a job, which was a miracle, and it was located somewhere I rather liked. So I'd work insanely hard and see what happened. They must have had some belief in my ability to perform since they hired me, right? I just needed to pretend I believed in my ability to perform too.

Fake it 'til you make it.

An hour later, a text arrived: my mother, asking me to bring her an outfit to wear to the reading. She was still at Damon's hotel and planning to shower and dress there. In typical Violet fashion, she'd detailed not only the specific items she wanted me to bring but also exactly where they were located. I gathered up the "citron sheath and beaded jacket, hanging in the closet, third from the left," as well as "the black Louboutin heels, in the bag beneath the net side of the suitcase" and packed them in the car. Then I took a shower and dressed myself for the reading in a long black blazer over a white tee, with jeans and boots. I braided my hair, added a pair of dangly silver earrings, and headed over to the hotel.

My mother answered the door in a robe, fresh out of the shower. She gave me a quick hug and returned to the bathroom, where she began applying her foundation layer. We were opposites where that was concerned; I applied the bare minimum in the morning—sunscreen, mascara, and tinted lip balm—and threw them back into the drawer, calling it done; she lugged around a bag full of makeup everywhere she went and could reapply completely at any time. Her readiness for potential adventure sharply contrasted my boring old expectation I'd be home again at night with no exciting activities for which I might need to refresh myself on the horizon. Le sigh.

Damon's hotel room was fairly spacious, with a neatly made king-sized bed in the center. A desk was positioned against the opposite wall, next to a dresser and a closed armoire that presumably held a television. The decor was brown and ivory, dotted with pictures of pottery and cactus flowers. I placed her dress carefully on the bed and settled in the corner wing chair.

"Did you have a nice night?" I asked my mother.

"Oh yes. I'd forgotten how lovely Damon is when he wants to be," she said, sounding like a schoolgirl in the throes of a crush. "Or maybe he's happier these days."

"Why?" I certainly hadn't seen the lovely side of Damon. Yet.

"Because of Mina, darling. I think fatherhood is good for him."

"Were Minerva and Damon married?"

My mother paused, an eyeshadow applicator in her hand, and smiled at me.

"They were never serious romantically. Just friends with

benefits. Until Mina was born. You know what I mean by benefits, right, Lila?"

"Yes, Mom. I know what you mean." Honestly. Sometimes she acted like I was a Puritan goodwife.

"Their friendship became even deeper, and they made good co-parents."

"So you knew Damon back then?"

"Oh, yes. But he was Minerva's. And after her overdose—she struggled with such an addiction to painkillers, you might remember—Damon withdrew from all of us for a very long time. It was only a chance encounter at the Met last year that put us back in touch."

"I'm sorry about Minerva," I said.

"You remember her, don't you, darling? Minerva was one of my dearest friends back in the day. She was such a vibrant being. She came to visit when Aunt Rose and Uncle Paul were still alive, just after Calista was born. Then again for Rose and Paul's funeral."

"I don't," I admitted. "I'm sorry." Calista was born two years before I was, and the period around my aunt and uncle's fatal car accident was hazy at best. I had seen countless photos of Minerva in magazines, of course—she was one of the original supermodels and her face was everywhere. She was known for her Amazonian stature and piercing glare.

"Mina favors her," my mother said, resuming her eye shadow application. "She could be a model as well."

"Yes," I agreed. "She doesn't look like Damon at all."

"Well," my mother said, "he may not be her father." She clapped her hand over her mouth.

I walked over to the bathroom and leaned against the doorframe. "What do you mean?"

"Nothing," she said, fumbling with her false eyelash case.

"Mom, you can't just drop that comment and tell me to ignore it." I reached out and touched her arm. "Please go on."

"Well," she said, applying glue to a strip of spiky long lashes and positioning it in place, "this has to stay between us, okay?"

"Of course."

She took a deep breath and let it out slowly as she turned to face me. Only one side of her beloved false eyelashes applied so far gave her a very *Clockwork Orange* look. I stifled a smile.

"This is for your ears only, Lila Annabel Maclean. Do you absolutely swear to keep it to yourself?"

"I swear."

"When she found out she was pregnant, I went to the doctor with her. The father was either Damon or a one-night stand she met at a club, whom she described only as 'a Hot French guy.' She decided to proceed as if it were Damon. She made me promise never to tell him, so I haven't."

"Wow," I said.

She let out another deep breath. "It feels good to say it out loud. I've been carrying that around for years. Damon has really been kind to Mina, so I think Minerva made the right choice."

"What about Mina?" I said. "Don't you think maybe you should tell her too?"

"When she's just been reunited with her father? She's happy, he's happy. It doesn't matter now."

"Yes, but..." I trailed off. We were dancing dangerously close to our own situation. No matter what I said next, it would sound as though I was talking about my own father. My mother had always flat-out refused to tell me who my father was. She said she had her reasons, but I didn't even know what they were. It was simply a topic she refused to address and something I could never understand. I wished there wasn't something so complicated between us. We were at an impasse.

A strange look passed over her face. A similar thought must have occurred to her.

"Anyway, darling," she said brightly, "Damon just called a few minutes ago. He went out to dinner with Mina and planned to go straight to the reading, but he forgot his briefcase, so they're going to swing back here and pick it, and me, up. Could you please set it on the bed?"

"Sure," I said. "Where is it?"

"In the closet."

I went over and pulled the double doors open. There were several suits and pants hung neatly on hangers. A closed brown leather suitcase was on the floor. I had to slide a few of the items to the left in order to see the battered briefcase on the floor—also in brown leather. The top was open, so I gently positioned the flap over the bag and picked the whole pile up rather than grabbing the handle. When I moved backwards, I bumped into my mother, who was heading toward her dress, and I lost my hold on the briefcase. The contents exploded onto the ground.

"Shoot," I said, bending down to scoop up the items. Knowing Damon, he'd probably accuse me of going through his things. So there was that to look forward to.

After I got the smaller items back inside, I turned toward the hundreds of pages which had spread out in ungraceful chaos all over the floor.

As I picked up the pages, I noted they were typed and double-spaced.

"Is Damon writing a new book?" I called out to my mom.

"Not that I know of." She paused in the act of donning her shoe, thinking. "Though we didn't really talk about his work. If you know what I mean."

"Mom, please."

She giggled. "You are so uptight, darling."

"Maybe. But still."

I had all of the pages together, so I tapped them gently on the floor to straighten the pile. I'd have to go through and put them in the correct numerical order. They had page numbers but no title or author's name listed in the header, the way one typically finds in a book manuscript. While I shuffled them into a neat stack, I looked into the closet interior again and froze.

Behind where the messenger bag had been sitting, there was something else. I hadn't seen it at first because it blended into the shadowy closet interior, but now that I was sitting, I could just make out a rectangular shape. I set down the stack of pages and reached into the dark closet to remove the object. It was an acrylic frame, around 9 x 12. I turned it over and gasped.

I held the title page of *The Medusa Variation*.

Damon had stolen his own manuscript from the library.

But why?

Soon afterwards, the door lock beeped and Damon strode inside. My mother was putting her "finishing touches" on in the bathroom, and I was sitting in the wing chair, putting the pages back in numerical order.

He froze when he caught sight of me.

"Hi Damon," I said, continuing with the work.

"What are you doing?" He tromped across the room and snatched the stack of pages from my hands. "These aren't yours."

"I'm sorry," I said. "They spilled on the floor and I was trying to reorganize them."

He scowled, looking down at the manuscript. "How did they spill?"

"I was pulling out the briefcase at my mother's request and—"

"Never mind," he snapped, then turned his bulk in the direction of the bathroom door and bellowed, "Violet, let's go."

"Is that the original manuscript of *The Medusa Variation*?" I asked. "Wasn't it stolen from the library? Did someone find it?"

Damon stroked his beard as he stared at me. "You ask a lot of questions."

I nodded.

"Suffice it to say I never gave the publisher permission to traipse the manuscript around the country, showing it off like some prize pig wearing a ribbon."

"Don't they own it, once you sign a contract?"

Damon snorted.

"Contract, schmontract."

That explained more about him than anything else he'd ever

said, frankly. I hoped my mother was hearing the conversation through the door. This guy was not someone to be trusted.

"How did you get it back?" I pressed, not willing to give up just yet.

"I took it," he said. His eyes bore into mine, challenging me to keep going.

"From the library?"

"No, from Jasper."

"Where did he get it?" I asked, genuinely surprised.

Damon shrugged.

"Did you at least contact the library to let them know it had been found? Or the chancellor? They have an agreement with the publisher—"

Damon stuffed the pages back into his briefcase and closed it. "Really not your problem, Lila."

I sputtered, indignant that he was treating the matter so lightly. Then again, he was a narcissist. He probably hadn't spent one second thinking about the other people involved in the manuscript's disappearance. I did not like this man spending time with my mother. But he was right—it wasn't my problem. Still, I could let Ruth know, in any case, that it had been found.

The bathroom door flung open and my mother emerged, freshly perfumed. The gardenia note hit me instantly even across the room. I stood up and moved toward the door.

"Would you mind putting these clothes in your car? I don't want to lug them around all day." She held out a neatly folded pile comprising yesterday's outfit.

"Sure," I said, receiving them on my upturned forearms.

"Thank you, darling. Mina's waiting downstairs—do you want to come with us?" She looked at Damon for confirmation.

"Or I could drive you all," I offered.

"Jasper has a car," Damon said curtly. "But before we go, I need to speak with you alone, Violet. If you don't mind, Lila." His tone implied that I had no right to mind and I had already overstayed my welcome. So I left.

Chapter 21

I parked in the lot near the English department—normally, I'd have walked from home—but my mother might need me to drive her after the reading. I wasn't sure what her plans were.

Calista happened to be passing by, so we made our way toward Brynson Hall together.

I admired the black beret Calista wore atop her blonde bob. I wasn't much of a hat person, and I respected those who could pull it off. It wasn't just a question of plunking a chapeau on one's head: there was a certain sort of insouciance necessary for beret-wearers, and my cousin had it in spades.

"What happened to you at the chancellor's party?" she asked.

"What do you mean?"

"After the whole thing with Damon, Nate was looking for you. Did he ever find you?"

"Yes," I said. "He and Amanda both did."

"I think he was jealous," she said, sounding delighted.

"About what?" I concentrated on the sidewalk, unsure if I wanted to participate in this conversation.

"Lex."

"Nothing to be jealous about. We barely had a chance to speak. Plus, Nate is dating Amanda—"

"What did you think of her?" Calista asked. "Isn't she great?"

If you liked overachieving sprites.

"But..." she continued, not waiting for me to answer. She

paused to say hello in response to a student who greeted her, then lowered her voice. "I don't think he wants to be with her."

"Hmmm."

"I mean," Calista said, warming up to her subject, "she's super smart, she's nice, and she's beautiful too."

"Right. Who would want to date someone like *that*?"

She laughed. "You know what I mean. She's perfect on paper, yeah, but he doesn't love her. There's chemistry, obviously, but it doesn't seem like true love."

"Maybe they're just having fun, Calista. Not everyone who dates is in love."

"True, but I think he's looking for love. And honestly, I think he has feelings for you." She stopped walking and turned to face me. "Do you have feelings for him too?"

"What? Nate? No. We're friends."

"I don't know. There's something in the air when you're together, some vibe that is palpable. You and Nate are soul mates, I think."

"You are such a romantic," I said, smiling at her earnest face. "And I appreciate that about you. But Nate and I are just friends. Seriously. I don't have time for any relationship things right now, anyway."

She waved that claim away. "There's always time for relationships."

"Seems like there's not even enough time for me to finish my work every day, much less date someone."

"Well, if he were interested, would you?"

"No, Calista. Please don't try to make anything happen. We're just friends. In fact, that's all I want us to be."

Her expression made it clear she doubted me.

"Wait, if you think Nate and I should be together, why did you invite Lex to the reception?"

She cocked a brow, her expression suddenly looking far less soft than just a moment before. In fact, she looked downright mischievous. "To make Nate jealous. Which I did."

"I may have underestimated you," I admitted.

"Most people do." She readjusted her beret. "By the way, Lex is not too shabby either."

I agreed with her, but I didn't want to discuss it right now. And luckily I had the perfect change of topic.

"Let's put a pin in that for now. I have to tell you something: you know how the manuscript went missing from the library? I just saw it—in Damon's briefcase."

"What? How did it get there?" She gripped my arm for a moment. "I don't understand."

"Neither do I. But he has it."

"So weird," she said. "Why would he steal it?"

"He didn't," I said. "Jasper did."

"Jasper?" Calista thought for a moment. "Why would he want it?"

"It's probably worth quite a lot of money."

"But if he was going to sell it, why would he have given it back to Damon?"

"Excellent point."

To ponder.

We walked through the double doors of Brynson Hall together. Francisco was standing near the hallway next to the main auditorium, where people were filing in to claim their seats, almost an hour early. Looked like this would be another sold-out event. He beckoned us over, a grim look on his face.

"Have you seen Damon?"

"He's on the way," I said. "He's walking over with Mina and Mom. They should be here any minute." My mother had promised to deliver him to the event without allowing him to stop for drinks, if that was on his itinerary. I knew she'd be successful at diverting him if need be. And she was clearly content to be shepherding him over to the reading. Although I couldn't understand her attraction to Damon, today there was a certain electric quality to her being. I guessed they had reaffirmed their fondness for each other—and if he made my mother happy, who was I to question his motives?

Except that I didn't want my mother to get hurt.

I decided to have a talk with her about Damon tonight. To express my reservations. Then she would go ahead and do whatever the heck she wanted to do anyway. That's how we did things.

"I hope he gets here soon," Francisco said. "We're running out of time."

I checked my new watch. "We still have forty-five minutes. Don't worry. And he might already be backstage. I had to park my car over by Crandall, so they may have beaten us both here."

We agreed that Calista would go and secure seats for us while Francisco and I went to look for Damon.

We searched everywhere with no luck, then Francisco showed me to the room where Damon had waited before his first reading.

"There's still a half hour," I said. "They'll be here." The sounds of audience members filling up the auditorium were muted by the cement walls, but the tranquility didn't have a calming effect on Francisco.

"This is a disaster," he said desperately. "If they don't show up, I'm done. The chancellor is already breathing down my neck about how everything is messed up. When I go up for tenure, I don't want to be engraved in the chancellor's memory as the candidate who humiliated Stonedale." Francisco and I looked at each other for a long moment, then he exploded into a string of colorful curses.

It was strange to catch a glimpse of Francisco's typically cool exterior crumble. He always gave the impression of being able to handle anything, albeit impatiently. I wondered if Calista had witnessed his vulnerable side very often.

"I'll call my mother," I said, already pressing her number in my contact list.

Her voicemail answered, so I left a message asking her to please text me the anticipated arrival time.

"At least we have good support in place," he said. "Both Campus Security and Stonedale PD are out there."

It was reassuring, though I fervently hoped tonight went off without a hitch.

A man in the familiar green facilities uniform poked his head into the room. "We can't get the microphone to work," he informed us. His nametag said "Gary."

Francisco resumed his swearing streak.

"Can I do anything?" I asked Gary.

"I can work on the electrical box, but we could try a different mic. There are a few more in the closet of the control booth—would you grab one?"

"Sure."

He nodded curtly and wiggled a key off of the silver ring holding about sixty keys. How he kept those straight, I had no idea. "Here you go. Get one from the shelf marked 'front stage.'"

I took off at a jaunty clip out of the waiting room, only to realize I didn't know where the control booth was. Sheepishly, I returned and asked for directions. It was in the auditorium proper, facing the stage—a glass booth along the back wall from which technicians ran the sound and lights for plays and musical performances. Simple events like readings could be handled backstage, but complex events required additional technologies. Gary added that the chancellor had paid extra to make sure the booth was completely soundproofed so there was no chance his wife Patsy had to suffer through the clicking of controls during her beloved chamber orchestra concerts.

Gary snorted when he said that.

I refrained from comment, which I thought was prudent.

As I walked down the stairs stage right, I saw my mother, Damon, Mina, and Jasper coming toward me. They were laughing about something.

"Lila, darling!" My mother hurried the last few steps and gave me a quick embrace. "Here we are, as promised." She whispered into my ear, "And I haven't let Damon have liquid of any kind."

"Great job, Mom."

I greeted the rest of the group and wished Damon good luck.

He touched his forehead in something between a salute and a hat tip and followed my mother up the stairs.

"Please thank the planning committee for making sure there's security here," Mina said. She grabbed my hand and put both of hers around it. "And thanks again for helping me on Sunday," she added under her breath. To my surprise, she pulled me into a brief hug as well, just as my mother had.

Whatever happened tonight, at least I'd been well-hugged.

"Would you like to watch with us from backstage?" Jasper asked. "It's a whole different experience."

"Thanks, but I'm going to sit with my friends. Just have to grab a microphone first." I pointed to the back of the auditorium toward the sound booth and waved the key.

"Is there something wrong with the sound system?" He looked slightly alarmed.

"They think the current mic is shot. No worries—they'll fix it up. They do it all the time," I reassured him. "Hey, can I talk to you afterwards?"

"About what?" Mina moved closer to him and put her arm through his possessively.

"Damon said you found his manuscript." I thought it wise to go with "found," rather than the more accusatory "stole."

Jasper stood perfectly still and blinked at me. It seemed, though it must have been an illusion, as if his blond spikes stood up slightly straighter too. I could see him struggling to decide how to respond.

"Isn't he the best?" Mina said, squeezing his arm. "My father was beside himself when that disappeared."

"Where was it?" I addressed Jasper again.

He didn't respond.

"The manuscript?" I prodded. "How did you find it?"

"Long story," he said after an extended pause, no doubt buying himself some time to think of a good answer.

"Well, congrats," I said cheerfully, looking down at the key in my hand, which reminded me I had been sent on a mission. "Speak

to you later? I really do want to hear more about the manuscript."
We agreed to meet after the reading out front.

Mina pulled Jasper toward the stage. He still seemed thrown
off by my question, stumbling as she tugged on his arm.

I walked up the aisle, spotting Calista on the far side of the
auditorium deep in conversation with Judith and Willa. Looked like
she had scored some great seats in the second row. I made a mental
note of her location so that I could find her once the crowd, which
was pouring in at a steady rate, was settled.

At last I reached the control booth. I fit the key into the lock; it
turned smoothly and clicked. The door swung open quietly, and I
felt around for a switch, which was right next to the door on my left.
When the overhead lights came on, I found myself in a long
rectangular space—something like mission control rooms I'd seen
on television—with three levels. The lowest level featured a long
board full of switches, buttons, and levers. A number of rolling
chairs were clustered together at the far end; I supposed they were
used to slide along the board as needed. Behind it was a row of
chairs bolted to the ground with an empty counter in front of them;
electrical outlets were spaced every so often, likely for laptops or
other equipment. The backs of the chairs had vertical metal bars—
very modern and clean design. The highest level was simply a flat
empty space that could presumably be adapted for whatever was
necessary. The second and third sections were divided by a waist-
high silver bar in a long "U" with squared edges, probably to keep
people from tumbling down from the third level.

The dark glass allowed technicians to keep the booth
illuminated inside during performances without bothering the
crowd, but the stage was perfectly clear from in here. I made my
way across the thickly carpeted floor until I located the closet along
the back wall. The door was locked, but my key worked there, too,
and I went inside. The closet ran the length of the booth and had
shelves along the walls filled with electrical equipment, most of
which I didn't recognize, all with cords coiled up around them. It
created a decidedly snake-like effect, and I shivered as I began to

move slowly along the shelves, looking for the label Gary had mentioned.

Then I heard the sound of the booth door closing and turned to see who would come through the open closet door. My body tensed completely. This place was creepy, and I wasn't expecting company.

Jasper entered the closet, and I jumped.

"Sorry. Gary sent me. I should have called out or something. Do you need some help?"

My shoulders relaxed. "Yes," I said. "Can you please help me find a shelf marked 'front stage'?"

"Sure. Which ones have you checked?"

"Only these two," I said, gesturing to the two behind me.

"I'll take the other side." We moved in tandem, in slow motion, all the way to the back of the closet.

"Got it." It was the last shelf on the bottom row on my side. I held the microphone in one hand and kept the key in the other to make sure I left with both of them.

"Great," Jasper said. I followed him back through the main area of the booth, but right before we exited, he spun around and blocked the door. "But unfortunately, I can't let you go out there."

Chapter 22

"Sit," he said, pointing to the second row of chairs bolted to the floor.

"I'm not going to sit! I'm leaving." I tried to slip around him to the right.

He lunged, grabbed me by the shoulders, and dragged me over to a chair. I struggled, but it all happened so fast that I couldn't do anything other than whack him with the microphone, which didn't seem to faze him. He bent my arms behind me and fastened my wrists with something that cut painfully into my skin. I tried to move, but he had secured me somehow to the vertical bars on the chair back that I had so recently admired.

"Help!" I screamed, leaning forward as far as I could, which wasn't much, and giving it all I had. "Help me!"

He ripped the mic and key out of my hand and came around in front of me, an odd look playing across his face.

"Gary said this booth is soundproofed. I don't think anyone can hear you."

I stared at him. "Jasper, untie me. Please."

"I can't. And I apologize if those plastic ties are too tight—I grabbed them from a box backstage, but there weren't any instructions."

"They're incredibly tight. They really hurt."

"I'm sorry, Lila."

Trying to ignore the burning in my wrists, I took a deep breath and attempted to reason with him. "Jasper, whatever you're doing can stop right now. Just let me go and we'll pretend this never happened."

"Can't do it. You know too much. This is for the best."

"Jasper, I don't know anything—not a single thing—so could you please let me go?"

"Well, I can't do that *now*," he said exasperatedly. "You'll tell everyone I'm a psycho."

"I swear I won't," I said. "It's just a misunderstanding. Between us. Never to be spoken of again."

The air was charged, to say the least. He pressed his lips into a thin line.

"Sorry."

"Can you at least tell me what's going on?"

"It's a long story," he said.

"I do not appear to be going anywhere," I said angrily.

He perched on the edge of the table. "I didn't mean for any of this to happen. That's the most important thing for you to know."

I assumed a pleasant, interested face, which was harder than it normally would have been, given the circumstances.

He leaned back on table and crossed his legs. "Damon is going to confess something tonight. Something important. Let's just say I need things to go the way they need to go." He paused for a moment, lost in thought. I wiggled my wrists experimentally, trying to be unobtrusive but he noticed, returning from his reverie.

"Stop it," he said coldly.

"Jasper, what does Damon's confession have to do with me?" I asked. "I don't know what you're talking about."

"But you asked about the manuscript—"

"All I know is that you gave him the manuscript."

He considered this. "That's part of it."

"Did you take it from the library?"

Jasper winced. "It was part of the deal. I didn't have any choice."

"You made a deal with Damon?"

Jasper scratched the back of his head but didn't say anything.

"What's the deal, Jasper? How did you get ahold of the manuscript?"

"I paid a student two hundred dollars to get it for me."

"But why?"

"All will become clear soon enough, Lila." He glanced at his watch. "Fifteen minutes until show time." He picked up the microphone and started toward the door.

I spoke softly. "Please let me go afterwards. Since the secret will be out."

He didn't respond.

At least I could see the stage from where I was sitting.

All tied up.

Jasper ripped off a piece of duct tape from a roll he materialized from somewhere. I quickly pointed out that he'd just said the room was soundproofed, but he came closer anyway. He placed it carefully over my mouth, explaining he couldn't have me making any noise while he slipped out the door. He managed to smooth it down firmly even though I was twisting my head from side to side.

I didn't want him to touch me.

He walked down to the first row of the booth and perused the panel for a moment, then pressed a button and the lights began to glow. Over his shoulder, he said, "I know how to work a board from undergrad. Mina and I both majored in theater. We really are a perfect fit, aren't we?"

I so did not care right now.

He pushed a few more buttons, sliding one switch toward the top of the panel.

"I want to make sure you can at least hear everything. It's going to be *epic*."

Then he was gone.

I stared at the control board, too far away for me to reach. Then, after a fruitless struggle to release my arms, which only made them ache in addition to the burn, I tried kicking the empty table in front of me. It thumped but didn't seem to do anything other than making my foot hurt. So I sat there, watching helplessly as audience members took their seats.

Francisco stood near the stage, talking to Gary. Jasper walked over and handed Gary the microphone. Gary switched it out with the one on the lectern. All three of them disappeared backstage. I could now hear the sounds of the audience members—distant and tinny but audible through the new mic.

Wait, was there a chance Francisco knew where I was? Had he been listening when Gary gave me the key? I couldn't remember where he was in relation to the original request. My brain seemed increasingly fuzzy. I didn't know if it was from fear or a lack of air. Duct tape on one's mouth is not only uncomfortable but also restrictive. I concentrated on breathing slowly through my nose in an attempt to slow my heartbeat. The last thing I needed right now was to have a full-on panic attack. Those were hideous enough even without being lashed to a chair and gagged.

My cell phone rang. Probably my mother wondering where I was. The ring tone stopped after a few repeats and I had an idea: if I could get the phone onto the floor, maybe I could press buttons with my feet.

I tried to lean over so the phone would fall out of my jacket—from the deep pockets I'd loved so much because they had a flap at the top to keep everything inside—but I couldn't get far enough horizontal to let it slide out. Finally, I had to admit defeat. All I could do was sit there and worry.

I worried about what Damon was going to confess.

I worried about my mother and what this would mean for their relationship.

I worried about what would happen to Mina when her father said whatever he was going to say.

I worried whether anyone would ever find me up here.

The sounds of the crowd grew louder, and my thoughts churned. If this were a play, the room would be swarming with technicians in charge of special effects. But readings only required regular lights and microphone, which were also controllable backstage. Maybe Gary would come looking for his key? Why hadn't he done that before, though, when Jasper handed him the microphone? Maybe he'd forgotten. Or maybe he didn't care. Maybe he was more focused on getting to the bar to hang out with his buddies after quitting time.

Curse you, Gary!

Chapter 23

The crowd fell silent when Francisco walked on the stage. He calmly greeted and thanked the audience members for coming—especially if they'd attended the other night. Smoothly, he gave the same introduction to the original reading, pausing for the chancellor's spiel in the middle as before. Then it was Damon's turn to come onstage. I had to give him credit for returning after the uncomfortable performance—some people would have cut bait and fled, or whatever the saying was. Perhaps he felt that if he was going to be paid, he should actually give the reading. Or perhaps he wanted to prove he wasn't the stumbling, slurring person who showed up last time. In any case, this Damon was already different, striding across the stage confidently—he didn't have his cane this time. He placed his book and reading glasses on the lectern and surveyed the crowd with a broad smile on his face.

"Hello, everyone" he said into the microphone. "Let's give this another try, shall we?"

A ripple of laughter cut through the audience.

"Last time, as you may or may not know, someone had taken it upon themselves to administer some medicine to me. And, well, you saw the effects. Not my best reading style," he said ruefully, rubbing his forehead.

There was more laughter.

"But I'll try to put everything to rights this evening. Thanks for giving me another chance."

The audience applauded.

Damon opened the book and removed a sheet of paper, which he unfolded. "In fact," he said, "I'm going to read something completely new. You'll be the first to hear it."

Louder applause.

"I'd like to invite some people to join me onstage." He gestured to someone in the wings, and two Stonedale facilities workers emerged carrying chairs. They placed them behind, and to the side of, the lectern. Damon, in the meantime, went over to the side of the stage and disappeared behind the curtain, reappearing quickly with Mina in tow.

As they walked, she looked uncertainly at him, and he nodded his head. She took a seat. Damon returned to the microphone. "This is Mina Clark, my daughter, who is, I'm proud to say, working on her MFA in creative writing."

The audience applauded wildly.

"Next, please welcome Jasper Haines, my future son-in-law." The audience applauded again as Jasper strutted—there was no other word for it—across the stage. He had a wide smile on his face and went straight for the other chair.

"Jasper is currently writing his dissertation on the books which have the grave misfortune to carry my name on them."

The audience applauded again.

"This is called 'The Author.'" He put on his reading glasses and began reading from the page now sitting on the lectern. "Once upon a time, there was a farmer in Iowa who wrote a novel. His name was Jasper Haines."

"This man," he held his arm out toward Jasper's chair, "is his grandson."

There was a flutter of reaction among the audience members.

Jasper's face was downright gleeful. Mina, on the other hand, stood and took a step toward the lectern. Damon put his arm out, low and to the side, his palm facing her in an unmistakable "stop" signal, and she froze, then sat back down in her seat.

Damon paused, removed his glasses, and continued to speak. He was no longer referring to the page he'd begun reading from.

"The first Jasper was my neighbor, and I sometimes helped him out on the farm—you know, feed the animals, rake up hay, stuff like that. He gave me some money for it, which as a grad student at the university, I really needed. He and his wife Vera were very good to me. I sat right at the supper table with them and their boy Junior night after night."

He paused. "Vera used to make these wonderful meals—pot roast, mashed potatoes, pie—the works. While Jasper and I worked outside around the farm, she would be in the kitchen for hours whipping up some mighty good eats."

The audience made appreciative sounds at his gustatory memories.

"As we worked, we often talked about books. Jasper had been a voracious reader since high school. I can remember being impressed with insights he shared about classical myth while we repaired a fence. He was a special fan of the Medusa myth—for him, it captured the dangers of looking truth in the face. In fact, he'd nicknamed the plane he flew in the war after her. Anyway, when I'd worked for them for over a year, Jasper surprised me. When I was leaving one night, he gave me a brown paper bag with a typed manuscript inside. He didn't say much other than that he wondered if I'd take a look; he was interested to hear what I thought. No one knew he wrote, he said. He didn't even know why he did it."

Damon took a breath.

"I was reluctant. I had been struggling with my own novel, which was due by the end of the month if I wanted to graduate. I only had nine chapters written, and I couldn't seem to go any further. But there was something in his eyes I could relate to...a need of some kind. I certainly understood the desire to have one's words read. So I agreed, warning him it would probably take several weeks or longer before I could get back to him. He said that wasn't a problem, whenever I got around to it."

Damon shifted his weight, gripping the side of the lectern with both hands. "When I began to read, I couldn't believe it. The book was amazing. I read the whole thing in a matter of days and raced over to the farm to tell him how good it was. Only—" He stopped.

I was so caught up in the story that I found myself leaning forward despite the restraints, as if it would make him continue.

He cleared his throat. "Jasper had died suddenly, in his sleep. One of those things, said the doctor. No explanation for it."

The audience responded with sympathetic noises. He scratched his head and stared down at the lectern, collecting himself emotionally. Finally, he looked up.

"We all grieved for him. Vera disappeared almost immediately—I think she and Junior went to live with her sister for awhile. It was a tragic thing, them being left suddenly like that, and I was glad they had family to take them in. I tried to decide whether to give her the novel or to respect Jasper's wishes and keep it a secret. I didn't know if he'd told her about it or not. Meanwhile, my advisor was pressuring me to submit a novel for the degree, and I didn't have enough money to pay any more tuition, so out of desperation, I typed up a new title page and turned the manuscript in under my own name."

There were gasps from the crowd. Damon began to speak faster.

"All I changed was the title, so that it foregrounded the plane. He'd given the colonel in the story the plane, so I knew it had meaning for him. Plus, as I said, we'd often talked about myths, and it made sense to infuse the title with more literary resonance. It wouldn't hurt anybody, I reasoned. Only my advisor and the other people on my committee would read it. This was long before the internet, back when final writing projects were just stored in file cabinets in a basement on campus somewhere. I'd be able to get out of town, degree in hand, and move on to the next chapter of my life. Maybe if I got a good job, I'd be able to send some money back to Vera, help her out now that Jasper was gone. I never knew anything would come of it, but my professor, unbeknownst to me, mentioned it to a friend who was an agent, and it had been accepted before I even knew it was submitted." He shook his head. "When the contract arrived, I signed, I'm sorry to say. I had no money. I needed the advance. I had absolutely no idea *The Medusa Variation* would become as significant as it did."

When he stopped speaking that time, the room was completely silent. I could feel the tension even through the walls of the booth.

"I became an important author, as they say. It all spun out of control very quickly. So I drank. And drank. And drank some more. But no amount of drink in the world can erase that kind of guilt."

The silence was shattered by widespread reaction. From my perch, I could see audience members turning to each other and discussing what they just heard. Some of them were motioning angrily. Others were shaking their heads. Jasper was sitting up almost preternaturally straight in his chair, straining to watch. I had to admire his restraint—he probably wanted to jump around the stage doing a victory dance. Mina remained seated with one hand over her mouth, motionless.

Suddenly, the door to the booth flew open.

"Hey! No one's supposed to be up here—" Gary marched in. "Oh, it's you, Professor," he said. For a split second, I thought he was a hallucination I'd conjured up through wishful thinking. When I squeezed my eyes shut, then opened them and he was still there, I was so relieved that tears sprang up immediately.

Something like "Mmmmpf!" came out as I tried to speak through the duct tape.

"You okay?" he asked, remaining by the door. I made another, louder unintelligible sound which prompted him into action. He raced over and ripped the duct tape from my mouth—which stung like anything—and peered into my eyes.

"Can you please untie me?" I begged him.

Gary pulled some silver instrument from his pocket and severed the ties in an instant. The worst pins-and-needle sensation I'd ever had flooded my arms at once, and I moaned.

"Should I call someone?" He was obviously concerned. "You hurt?"

"I'm fine," I said, gently rubbing my arms for a minute to get the circulation flowing. Then I lightly pressed the area around my mouth to counter the sting factor, which helped somewhat. "And I have to go, but thanks so much for rescuing me."

"You gotta call the police."

"I will. Bless you, Gary." I hobbled out of the booth and moved slowly down the side of the auditorium. It was too late for me to intervene with the reading, obviously, but I wanted to find my mother and let her know what was going on.

When I was about halfway down the aisle, Damon leaned closer to the microphone and said, "But there's more."

Chapter 24

I froze, just like everybody else.

"A few years ago, *this* Jasper Haines came to me." He pointed to the man sitting on the stage. "Turns out he'd learned his grandfather was the one who wrote the novel."

Jasper looked self-righteous.

"Yet rather than coming clean right away, which I volunteered to do—I was ready to be done with the whole thing—he had another idea."

A flash of panic crossed Jasper's face. "Damon, wait a minute!" he yelled. "We agreed—"

But the author plunged ahead. "He had written a little book, he said, that demonstrated a literary theory he'd been toying with. He wanted me to publish it under my name. I resisted at first, I did. But he said if I would go along with his idea, we wouldn't have to correct the first theft. He wanted to write his dissertation on both *The Medusa Variation* and the second one which would guarantee not only the completion of his doctorate but also, probably, a good job afterwards."

Damon shook his head and looked at Jasper, who had gone limp in his chair, his eyes closed.

"I absolutely did not want to go along with it, but I could understand this would give the kid a chance at success. If his grandfather's name had been on *The Medusa Variation* as it should have been, he might have had a better life to begin with. And it was my fault. So I agreed."

He put both hands over his face for a moment, then slowly rubbed his eyes. When he spoke again, his face was grim. "But then I had to embark on a book tour and claim words that were not mine for the second time. I did everything I could to stop the tour—I misbehaved whenever possible."

Mina stood up in her chair and went over to him. "Stop, Dad," she said gently, but loud enough that the microphone picked it up. "It's enough already. We all heard what you said—you were blackmailed into it. It's not your fault."

"There's more, Mina," Damon said. "I need to tell the whole story so we can be done with this." He caught her hand and escorted her back to the empty chair. She sank into it.

He returned to the lectern and leaned forward again. "Minerva Clark had lived next door to me and been my best friend for decades. When Mina was born, we all spent a great deal of time together until Mina went off to boarding school, which was the end of our family unit. Years passed, and Mina showed up in New York to attend graduate school after her mother had died. She told me her mother had confessed I was her real father."

He paused, looking at Mina. "This young woman has been a terrific companion to me, and I have enjoyed every minute of it."

Mina smiled at him. But it was a tentative kind of smile, as if she sensed that the other shoe was about to drop.

And then it did.

"But, unfortunately, she is not my daughter."

Mina spluttered and shook her head. "Dad, what are you talking about?"

He turned to her. "I'm sorry, Mina," he said sadly.

Damon addressed the audience. "Minerva and I had been involved at one point, it's true. But by the time Minerva met Mina's father, who was a married man in a very prominent political position, we were just friends, contrary to what everyone else thought. Minerva never told the father she was pregnant, but I was there for everything—the pregnancy, the birth, and for many years afterwards. I loved Mina as my own as a result of all the time we'd spent together when she was young, so it seemed like a small and proper thing to take her in when she appeared on my doorstep."

"You're *not* his daughter?" Jasper yelled at Mina.

Mina whipped her head back to Jasper and glared at him with such intensity that he jolted backwards, almost falling out of his chair.

"Didn't you hear him? I thought I was."

Damon leaned on the lectern, twisted around to observe the exchange.

Jasper recovered his balance and stood up. "You liar!"

Mina rose as well and slapped him across the face.

Jasper put a hand to his cheek and raised his other hand as if to slap her back but then froze as a piercing, agonized wail filled the auditorium, seeming to start in the back and snake through the crowd toward the front. Everyone turned in their seats, craning their necks to find the source of the sound. I swept the rows of chairs with my eyes, ultimately making out a tall figure leaning along the back wall of the auditorium. The wail stopped abruptly and the figure proceeded down the center aisle, gradually revealing a tall, stately woman. Her gray hair, steel-colored suit, and noble carriage gave the impression of being clad in armor. She climbed up to the stage, ignoring the three people populating it, and went directly to the lectern. Damon moved aside, as if pulled by an invisible force.

"Allow me to introduce myself," she said, her voice strong and clear. "I am the true author of *The Medusa Variation*."

An uproar swept the room. If this had been a Victorian novel, somebody would have swooned. Francisco strode out onto the stage and covered the microphone with his hand while he spoke in an urgent manner to the woman in gray and to Damon, who both stepped backwards to make space for him. After a few minutes, he leaned into the microphone.

"Ladies and gentlemen, we have an unexpected addition to our reading. Please welcome Vera Haines."

There was a spatter of applause. I joined in, feeling dazed.

She inclined her head slightly in his direction and returned to the lectern. Her body was rigid, and she looked ready for battle.

"I wrote the novel. No one besides my Jasper knew I was the author. I typed in the barn at night sometimes when I couldn't sleep. It took me two years to write the book and Jasper kept begging me to let Damon to read it. I refused. I didn't want anyone to know. I wasn't sure why I wrote it in the first place, other than I had a need to say something about the war that had changed Jasper so dramatically. Before he went, he was a happy man, full of life, content with his lot. We had been married the year before he finished college, and every day felt like a gift."

She paused for a moment, a slight smile on her face, at the thought of those days.

Then her mouth turned grim again.

"But when he graduated, he had to serve during the last two years in Vietnam. And when he came home, he was so different. Haunted. Like a ghost. He told me things that...well, I felt so helpless. After a few years, I started to write something to...to get the feelings out somehow. To try and make something good out of something so awful. And when Jasper read it, he just stared at me. Finally, he said it was exactly what he would have said about the war if he could. Thank goodness one of us could write, he said. From that point on, he was always after me to submit it to a publisher, but I just couldn't bring myself to do it. To me, it was private. I'd written it for him. But the more Damon was around the farm, the more Jasper became convinced he should read it. Damon was a few years younger than Jasper—same age as me, in fact—but Jasper was completely impressed with the whole notion of graduate school. They talked about literature for hours together, and he believed in Damon's knowledge. You'd have thought Damon was some sort of god," she said bitterly, looking at him with disgust.

"So I let him give the manuscript to Damon, as long as Jasper said he'd written it."

There was a long pause.

"Then my Jasper died."

The audience responded instantly, murmuring among themselves. Vera watched them for a moment, then lifted her chin and continued, "I had a nervous breakdown. I just collapsed, inside and out. I spent a few years in the hospital, and by the time I returned home, the book was out there in the world under Damon's name. I was furious, of course, but I didn't know what to do. People already stared at me oddly—this was small-town USA, you understand, and people who went to mental hospitals weren't treated like your average citizen. It took me a long time to get my son back. It was hard enough to fit back into my community—the looks some people gave me I wouldn't wish on my worst enemy. I knew no one would believe me if I started talking about being the real author of a famous book on top of *that*." She threw her hands up into the air.

"Then my grandson," she turned and gazed at him, "told me about writing his dissertation on the book he loved it so much. I like to think that maybe, on some level, he recognized my voice inside the story. And I realized here was a chance, at last, for me to give my husband some of the glory he so dearly deserved for what he'd been through for his country. And for me. So I told Jasper his grandfather had written *The Medusa Variation*. I believed he would do the right thing with that information. He's a smart boy."

Vera faced the audience again. "However, to my dismay, instead of simply debunking Damon and putting his grandfather's name on the manuscript, nothing happened. He didn't tell anyone. I didn't know he had concocted an even larger self-serving plan until tonight. Jasper, how could you?"

He looked crestfallen. His blond spikes might even have drooped.

"Then I watched Damon Von Tussel go through a completely new cycle of celebration for having produced yet another book—I was pulling my hair out, I'll tell you that much. And now I hear the second book was *also* written by a Haines?" She smacked the lectern, and everyone jumped. "Enough!"

"But Grandma—" Jasper began, moving toward her.

"Don't 'Grandma' me, young man. Sit down," she said. "All of this ends now. I don't know what will happen for you now that the truth is out. Some people find pleasure in other people's misfortune, so who knows? But make no mistake: it's repulsive. Every part of it. And the world will deal with you accordingly."

She turned to Mina. "I fear you have greater problems than this, and I hope you sort them out."

She faced Damon. "I've thought about this moment for a long time," she said slowly. "I've imagined over and over again what I would say to you about stealing my book and about dishonoring my husband's name. Or, actually, mine. But listening to you talk about it tonight, I think you've genuinely suffered. There will be more to come, unfortunately. But at least you did finally come forward and admit you'd done wrong. Thank you for that."

Damon swiped at his eyes roughly. "I'm sorry," he said.

She studied his face, then nodded curtly.

The audience gave her a standing ovation.

After the highly animated crowd had dispersed, I was sitting in the front row of the auditorium, watching Lex talk to Damon onstage. He'd come for my statement eventually; he knew Jasper had been responsible for whatever it was called when someone tied you to a chair in a sound booth against your will. I didn't want to press charges—but I would explain what happened.

Tally Bendel stomped up to us, waving her cell phone, which was ringing. She paused to see who was calling, then angrily stabbed the screen.

"Violet, call me when you're back in New York. Let's go to lunch and vent. I can't believe how many years I've had to put up with this son of a—"

"You've been a saint, it's true," my mother said quickly.

"You too, doll," Tally said. "Time for both of us to quit it." Her phone began ringing again, and she made a *tsk* of annoyance as she checked the screen and held up one finger. "Gotta take this one. See you in the city." She pointed at my mother and wheeled around to leave, her oversized bag flying out in an impressive arc.

"She's right, you know. To think how much time I spent praising his writing," my mother hissed out of the side of her mouth in an angry whisper. "That's what you have to do when you date an author, you know."

I decided now was not the time to make the obvious comparison to those who date artists.

She turned one of her bracelets around her wrist as she continued into a refrain I'd heard before. "Although artistic types do need some appreciation, it's true. One does hope for the tiniest morsel of encouragement after putting your art into the world, darling. After all, it takes every ounce of creativity and determination."

I gave the traditional response—"you're right"—to this comment. Next up on the familiar playlist was the disproven but still repeated Why It Doesn't Matter If No One Likes Your Work. She had produced variations of these ideas—minus the Damon aspect—as far back as I could remember. Which topic was rehearsed depended on where my mother was in the artistic process. I knew she had just completed an installation, so she was in the I Did My Best And That's All Anyone Can Do phase that accompanied letting go of her latest project.

I gave her a quick side hug.

A flurry of movement caught my eye. Jasper and Mina emerged from the wings. He was escorted by a tall police officer, and she trailed behind. The officer called over to Lex, saying something I couldn't quite make out. Lex nodded. The officer aimed Jasper into a chair not far from where we were sitting.

I stood, went to the edge of the stage, and looked up at Jasper. Even though he'd recently manhandled me, I wasn't scared of him, and I still had questions. Tall Officer hovered nearby.

"Are you okay, Jasper?"

He grimaced. "I'm sorry about the booth, Lila."

I dipped my chin, registering the apology.

"This was never about you...you just got caught in the middle of it." His lips tightened. "You heard what Damon said, but it all came from a good place, I swear. I had vowed to get revenge on Damon for having ripped off my grandfather. But I didn't want to just blurt it out—accuse him face to face. I wanted to humiliate him in front of an audience. I also wanted to make sure a correction was made, that the name Jasper Haines would be reinstated, connected, forevermore, with one of the most celebrated novels of the twentieth century. Grandfather would have wanted it, right?"

"So you tried to use your own fraud to expose his?" I wondered if he saw the irony in his plan.

"No. I wanted to rip off his effing mask and expose him for the viper he really is."

Apparently, he didn't see the irony.

"Does your dissertation expose Damon?"

"Yes and no. As it stands, it's an examination of personae in both *The Medusa Variation* and *In Medias Res*. That's what my committee saw and what was submitted to the university press. Purely literary analysis. But the final chapter, which I've already written, had to wait to go into the manuscript until Damon publicly stated his crime. That explains everything from my insider perspective and will increase the value of the study enormously."

"Ah," I said. Intentionally non-judgmentally.

Jasper grinned, surprising me.

"I can't wait to be done. I've spent years working on this project. You know what it's like to write a dissertation. Grueling and all-consuming. No matter how much you love the subject matter."

He appeared to have rebounded from having been exposed to the world as a blackmailer in a surprisingly short period of time, acting as if now he'd just go back to school and pick up where he left off.

"My defense is scheduled for next month," he said. "I am so ready."

What? His dissertation defense was likely the least of his

worries at this point. It didn't seem to have occurred to him yet that there were more pressing defenses in his future.

"Back to Damon for a minute—were you planning to kill him?"

"No way." Jasper shook his head vehemently. "Why would I kill him? I want him to suffer the humiliation. To do penance. To live as long as possible enduring the mockery and rejection of others who have learned the truth. Wishing him a long and miserable life, actually."

He didn't seem to register that his own part in the story was something not many people would celebrate either. Lex gestured to the front of the stage and Damon followed him. Another officer came out of the wings with a folding chair, which she set up neatly across from Jasper's. Damon was invited to sit.

"So we have ascertained that Jasper Haines's grandfather was the original author of *The Medusa Variation*," Tall Officer said.

"Grand*mother*," said Lex. "It was Vera."

The officer snapped his fingers. "That's right. I forgot. Sorry. But in any case, Mr. Von Tussel is not the author."

Damon didn't say anything.

Tall Officer continued, "So neither of the books which have your name on them were written by you."

Damon nodded, looking weary.

Lex jumped in. "Let's cut to the chase, if we can. The books, at this point, are not the focus of our investigation. Lawyers will sort that out. What we are trying to clarify at the present time is who is responsible for tampering with the spotlight thrown onto Mr. Haines, the drugging, and the attack by statue."

No one spoke.

Mina, who had been standing off to the side, moved in between the chairs and said, "Jasper, it's time to come clean."

His head swiveled so fast it seemed to blur. "What are you talking about?"

"Babe, just tell the truth." She wiped a tear from her eye and smiled weakly at him. "We all know you did it. It will feel better to admit it, and we'll be able to help you."

"Me? You're the one who should come clean—sounds like you were scamming Damon the whole time. At least I was honest with him."

"*Honest* with him? You stole the manuscript so you could sell it! You knew it would be worth more after you exposed him."

"Technically, I didn't steal it. I paid a student to take it for Damon. I was just the middleman," Jasper protested. "And if I were going to sell the manuscript, I wouldn't have given it back to him, which I did. It was part of our deal. He wanted to destroy it before it went on perpetual tour as evidence of the world's longest-running plagiarism case or something."

She shook her head and locked eyes with Tall Officer, then gave a tiny shrug, her hands palm up, as if to say *what can you do with a guy like this?*

"I'm going to need the name of that student later," Lex said.

Jasper ignored him, focusing on Mina.

"Please explain why I would want to be hit by a spotlight. It almost killed me!"

"It was the perfect way to point suspicion elsewhere and gain attention for Damon's reading. You could play the victim and soak up the sympathy. Meanwhile, you were plotting the next thing."

"Which was what?" Jasper asked. "Seriously, think about it. Why would I drug Damon? I wanted him to give a successful reading so he would confess. That was the whole point."

"Again, for publicity," Mina said. "I'm just glad you'll be behind bars so you can never hurt my father again."

"He is *not* your father. You're delusional," Jasper said, his face bright red, "and I didn't do anything wrong."

"You just admitted that you stole the manuscript from the library," Mina said exasperatedly.

"That's true," Jasper admitted. "But I didn't do anything else."

"Well, let's see...you blackmailed my father and you kidnapped Lila."

"I don't know if I'd call it kidnapping," I protested.

"Well, you were tied up," Mina snapped at me, eyes blazing.

"That's true," I agreed.

"So you've done plenty," she said to Jasper. "Don't you understand right from wrong?"

"Look," Jasper said, in a placating manner. "My part in this was to rectify an injustice. What's done is done. Damon has confessed and we can all move on."

"You don't *get* to move on," Mina said, her eyes wide. "You're done too." She addressed Lex. "Jasper doesn't know this, but the final chapter of his dissertation—the one calling my father a fraud, the one he planned to submit after tonight—has already been deleted from his computer, flash drive, and email as of this morning. He could write it again, of course, but I doubt his committee, or the university press for that matter, is going to be interested in his dissertation at all once they hear about how he blackmailed someone into participating in a plagiarism scheme for *In Medias Res*."

"You deleted it? How could you?" Jasper yelled. "You bitch!"

"Do *not* call me that," Mina yelled back. "And you cannot profit from what you've done!"

Lex looked back and forth between them, then held his hand up authoritatively. "Okay, let's take everything down a notch here. Let's start with the statue and work our way backwards."

I thought back to the Valentine's Day party, remembering the way the statue came crashing down. And before I knew it, I was on my feet yelling too.

"No—wait! He didn't do it!"

Everyone turned to me and the room fell silent.

Lex gestured for me to go on. His blue eyes were fixed on mine.

"He couldn't have done it. I was standing by the fountain right before the bust fell. And I saw Jasper go out the front door toward the valet station."

"But no one came down the stairs," Lex said.

"Correct," I said to him, then turned to address Mina. "Because you and I found the elevator together before that."

"I don't know what you're talking about," she said. Her lips were pressed together in a thin line.

"When we were upstairs, remember? We talked about the wallpaper inside the elevator? And you said it was...what was the word you used? Oh, right: you said it was 'fancy.'"

She shrugged. "Whatever. We saw an elevator. That was earlier, Lila. When the statue fell, I was in the same room as your mother, and we went to find Damon together."

"Except," I heard my mother say clearly from behind me, "we *weren't* together in the same room." She came over and stood next to me, resting her elbows on the stage. "Now that Lila mentions it, I distinctly remember admiring how the wallpaper inside of the elevator had the same bronze tones as your hair the way the overhead light shone on it, which means you must have been standing inside when the doors opened."

Mina opened her mouth, but no words came out.

"And afterwards, when you said you were pushed down the stairs. You made that up, didn't you? No one actually saw it happen," I said.

"But it did—" she began.

"It's about the money, isn't it?" I cut her off. "All the talk about wanting to preserve your father's legacy was really about the inheritance you thought you were getting. Keeping his reputation intact would ensure you were set for life. On the flip side, if he were exposed, the money would surely be in question, especially once the legal action kicked in. That's why you didn't want either Jasper or Damon to speak in public. At least until you'd convinced Damon not to confess...or so you thought. You started with the spotlight, didn't you? To keep Jasper quiet?"

She shook her head emphatically. "No!"

"Come to think of it," Damon said slowly, standing up. "The night of the panel, you said you were going to take a nap in the room you shared with Jasper before the dinner party. You had a migraine, you said. The inn was so close to campus—you could easily have made it there and back before Francisco and Lila came to pick us up. I would never even know you'd left. Plenty of time to pitch a light onto Jasper and run back."

"Jasper told me you majored in theater, Mina," I added. "You're a good actress—actually, a great one. I really thought you'd been pushed down the stairs. And with the theater experience, you certainly would know your way around a catwalk, I'd wager."

"You could have killed me," Jasper added angrily. "Or Damon, with the drugs."

"You're the one who has a prescription for Xanax, not me." She pointed to him. Apparently, she was sticking to her story. "You know those anxiety attacks you had last fall? You said they were about your dissertation, but maybe it was from all the plotting and scheming. Your conscience was trying to tell you something."

He stared at her. "I do have a prescription," he said slowly.

She smiled triumphantly at Lex. "See? I guess it's pretty clear what really happened here."

"Wait, how do you know about that, anyway?" Jasper pressed her.

"You told me about the attacks."

"No," he said, narrowing his eyes at her. "I mean about the meds. I never used them after the first time. They made me too groggy to write. How do you know I had them?"

"I happened to see a bottle in the back of your medicine cabinet."

Jasper threw up his arms. "Well, I didn't bring any with me."

"But *you* did," I interjected, speaking directly to Mina. "Right? Would have been easy to pocket some pills in case you needed them."

"I would never drug my father," Mina said coldly.

"But I'm not your father," Damon reminded her, matching her tone. "And you knew I wasn't."

"Why do you say that?"

"Those endless questions about the books and royalties...did you think you were being subtle?"

"I just wanted to know where things stood. I was trying to help you." Mina looked wildly around the stage, her eyes welling with tears. "I can't believe you're all accusing me."

Damon stared at her until her shoulders slumped.

"All I have ever done was look out for you," she said to Damon reproachfully, wiping a tear from her cheek.

"You mean you were looking out for your inheritance," he corrected her, shaking his head. "The one you thought you were getting, anyway."

"This is ludicrous," Mina protested. "You've all lost your minds."

"Ms. Clark, we need to finish this conversation down at the station," Lex said, walking toward Mina, handcuffs at the ready.

Time to leave. I turned, took two steps, and bumped into the chancellor's expensive suit—my face firmly planted into his chest.

"Oof," I heard him say above me.

I apologized, cheeks aflame, and propelled myself backwards.

He relocated himself to a safer distance by the first row of seats and beckoned me over. "Walk with me, Dr. Maclean," he commanded, moving briskly toward the center aisle.

My heart plunged straight into my boots.

He was going to fire me.

I followed reluctantly, wondering how I would ever find another position for next fall at the tail end of the academic hiring cycle.

The chancellor walked halfway up the aisle and stopped to face me.

"A student complaint came across my desk earlier this week," he said, waiting for acknowledgment.

"I know which one you mean." Simone must have convinced Stephanie Barnes to go through with it.

The chancellor rubbed his chin thoughtfully. "It's a tricky situation since the student in question is related to one of our most generous donors."

Dang. Here it came.

"I read carefully through the report you had filed with student judicial. Thing is—" He paused for a long moment, during which perspiration emerged from every pore in my body.

"—I agree with you."

You could have knocked me over with a quill.

"Especially in light of this," he said, as he gestured toward the stage. "Stonedale needs to stand firm against academic dishonesty."

He must have been worried about how it looked to the rest of the world that we'd invited a scoundrel to be our author of the week.

"I agree," I said, surreptitiously wiping the panic-sweat off my forehead.

"I wonder if you might be interested in joining a new task force to be charged with developing publicity-friendly anti-plagiarism slogans to raise awareness. Stonedale could become quite a leader in this area if we do it right."

I said I'd be delighted to serve on the Everyone Knows Academic Dishonesty Is Wrong But Here's Yet Another Reminder Committee.

I didn't say it like that, though.

"Thank you very much, Chancellor, for your support."

"Of course," he said loftily. "We do strive to support our professors."

The ones they liked anyway. Wait, did this mean the chancellor and I had turned the corner on our previously vexed relationship?

"I can't tell you how relieved I am," I said. "I thought you were going to—" I stopped myself.

"Going to...what?" he asked gently, his mouth curving in a tiny smile. A smile? We were definitely having a moment. Go for it.

"I thought you were going to fire me," I confessed, with a little nervous laugh.

"Oh. Well." He waved his hands in front of his chest as if erasing our budding connection. "We'll have to see how things go from here, won't we?" He strode back toward the stage, leaving me standing there with a jumble of emotions.

I may have—stupidly—just put the idea into his head, but I wasn't getting fired today.

Take that, Simone.

Chapter 25

The next afternoon, Calista and I met for coffee at Scarlett's. My spirits had been lifted by the sunshine on the way over, and I bounded into the café in a most unprofessorial manner, throwing my arms around my cousin and giving her a hug.

"What was that for?" she asked, laughing. She readjusted the collar of her sage sweater coat and waited, looking quizzical.

"Well, Arts Week is done, for one thing. And we figured out what's been going on—as I texted you, it was Mina all along."

"Yes, I want the scoop, but let's order first. I'm starving." She swept me in line for the counter. "Did Aunt Vi leave?"

"Yes, this morning. Sorry that you and Francisco didn't get our voicemail about joining us for dinner last night."

"Me too," Calista said, looking glum. "I was recharging my phone. Stupid battery. Though Francisco was crushed by Damon's revelations, so it's probably better we stayed away from other humans."

"Well, at least you got to see her during the visit. And she gave me a thousand not-so-subtle hints about improving my tiny house with fabulous art. I'd be happy to share."

Calista smiled. "Well, if there's one area she knows...."

"Indeed."

"Is she still going to date Damon?"

"She mentioned something about how he really was a bit old for her. Which in Violet code, as you know, means curtains for that relationship. In addition to Damon turning out not to be a writer after all, I suspect she's also angry he didn't confide in her about Mina's real father. Minerva had fed Mom some story about what she called 'a Hot French Guy'—"

A flash of annoyance crossed her face. "What? Why didn't she tell me?"

"There was no time—"

Calista crossed her arms over her chest in a kind of nonverbal harrumph.

"She would have told you too, if you'd been there yesterday," I assured her. "Anyway, it's a moot point now that it turned out to be a lie. There was no Hot French Guy. Or if there was, he wasn't the father. As Damon said last night, it was someone in politics. Mina admitted to Lex later after much questioning that she had actually known who her real father was. All the insistence onstage about how she thought it was Damon? Huge lie. She was scamming him, as he suspected. And once Lex was able to obtain the Big Truth, the rest was easy to sort out."

"Ooh, how did you find out?"

"Lex called last night." I'd pressed for details on the case, but he'd only confirmed the paternity thing, which may have been unintentional as he tried to dodge my barrage of questions while simultaneously helping me understand that I was not an official member of the crime-solving team. Even though I'd solved the crime. And yes, I had reminded him of that little fact. "I don't know if I'm technically supposed to have the information about the paternity thing, so maybe don't repeat it."

Calista made a zipping gesture across her mouth and threw an imaginary key over her shoulder.

"I think it's pretend to lock your mouth and throw away a key *or* do the zipper thing. I don't think you can mix and match."

"But you know what I mean, right?"

"Yes."

"So I do it how I do it," Calista said, shrugging. "Okay?"

I laughed. "Carry on."

"Anyway, poor Aunt Vi. She and Damon were cute together."

Boy did we ever have different readings of Mr. Von Tussel. I was thrilled my mother was breaking up with him.

"Don't worry about her, Cal. She has many admirers, as you know."

We placed our orders, paid for our drinks, and moved to the pick-up area.

"I'm not worried about her," she said. "I'm just sad they reconnected and it turned out not to mean anything. I just want Aunt Vi to be happy."

"I don't know," I said slowly. "Sometimes the reconnection is the meaningful part all by itself."

Calista brightened. "That's true."

"How's Francisco? He seemed upset last night."

That was stating it mildly. I'd seen him storm up the aisle of Brynson Hall immediately after the reading was over, Calista trailing behind.

"He's fine. It took all night to calm him down though. After a long rant, he realized his book was still viable. He just had to add a prologue explaining that the authorship had changed. The texts, though, remain the same, so his analysis should still hold. He wasn't doing biographical criticism, thank goodness."

"What's going to happen to Jasper's book?"

She shrugged. "No idea. What about Damon's? I mean, his entire authorial reputation just vanished into thin air."

"You're right. But Mom said he had already called his publisher and was making arrangements to have *The Medusa Variation* published under Vera's name. And there will be no more copies of *In Medias Res* printed. Ever."

"What will happen with royalties and so forth?"

"I don't know. I'm sure there will be a great deal of litigation in his future."

Calista sighed. "You know the original books, with the fraudulent name on the cover, will become the editions that collectors will seek out."

"That's just wrong, isn't it?" I said. "But, again, you're right."

"Tell me more about what happened after the reading," she said.

"Basically, Mina blamed Jasper for the spotlight, the drugging, and the statue. He said she was lying and blamed her right back," I told Calista.

She shook her head. Her blonde bob stayed in place admirably. "I'm assuming the engagement is off, then."

"Most definitely," I said, laughing.

"So Damon plagiarized one book, Jasper blackmailed Damon into plagiarizing a second book, and Mina did the rest? Do I have it right?"

"Pretty much, though Jasper also stole the manuscript from the library—well, he paid a student to snag it—at Damon's request. Damon didn't want the manuscript traveling around with his name plastered onto the front page. He was ready to be done with the whole thing and knew he was going to confess all along, regardless of what Mina said."

"But how did you figure it out?"

"I realized not only that Jasper couldn't have had the statue because I'd seen him walk out the front door seconds beforehand, but also that all of the attacks, or whatever you want to call them, had the same motive: to prevent the truth from being told. Mina needed Damon's reputation to stay intact in order for her inheritance to be worth something, and once she'd read Jasper's final chapter—which he didn't know she'd read—she must have realized what was about to happen. She didn't want to take a chance on Jasper saying anything at the panel, so she clocked him with the light. She didn't want Damon to say anything at his reading, so she drugged him, then followed up with the statue on top of it, perhaps in an effort to scare him from reading at all...or to give him a concussion...or to kill him." I shivered.

"But why did she not do something before the second reading?"

"It appears she has strong convictions in the power of her own persuasion, or at least that's how my mother described it."

"Must be nice," Calista said sarcastically.

"This part is a little blurry." I'd pieced it together from bits and pieces that Lex had tried not to share with me during my questionfest. "Not sure when exactly Mina told Damon she was aware of his fraud, but she definitely thought she'd talked him out of confessing."

"Hmm. Do you think Mina really loved Jasper?" Of course my cousin would zone in on the romantic aspect of the situation.

I shrugged.

"Wow. Reminds me of my stories," she said, her eyes shining. Since high school, she'd been addicted to one of the longer-running soap operas. Though I wasn't a fan myself, I'd listened to her talking about it enough to understand her point, so I nodded in confirmation. "Mina's a piece of work, isn't she?"

"They all are. Oh, and I think she also sent the threatening emails that we all got, telling us to cancel—"

"Or else." Calista finished the sentence for me in an ominous tone. "Why did we all freak out, anyway? It's so vague."

"Maybe it's the vagueness of the threat that makes it potent in the first place."

"I suppose. But why do you think Mina sent the emails?"

"It wouldn't make any sense for Jasper to have done it...he *wanted* Damon to confess. She's the only one who had a motive."

"So awful." My cousin shook her head. "What a horrible person. It's kind of shocking...she didn't seem like a criminal."

"Well, technically all three of them all are criminals. I have a feeling it's going to take the courts a long time to sort this out."

She raised her eyebrows.

At the same moment, I heard the bells on the door jingle, and Calista's face lit up in response to whatever she saw behind me.

I turned around to see Nate waving.

"Oh yeah, I forgot to tell you. I think he and Amanda broke up last night," Calista said quickly. "We walked past them after the reading, and they were arguing about something right there on the sidewalk. It didn't sound good."

I kept smiling, though it felt awkwardly plastered on as I processed what she had said. I didn't know what the break-up meant, but I was surprised to realize a sort of relief at the news. I waved back at him.

As Nate moved toward us, the bells rang again, and Lex stepped over the threshold. He tipped his head up slightly in greeting, his eyes locked on mine.

This should be interesting.

Cynthia Kuhn

Cynthia Kuhn writes the Lila Maclean Academic Mystery Series. Her work has appeared in *McSweeney's Quarterly Concern, Literary Mama, Copper Nickel, Prick of the Spindle, Mama PhD* and other publications. She teaches English at Metropolitan State University of Denver and serves as president of Sisters in Crime-Colorado. For more information, please visit cynthiakuhn.net.

Henery Press Mystery Books

And finally, before you go...
Here are a few other mysteries
you might enjoy:

TELL ME NO LIES

Lynn Chandler Willis

An Ava Logan Mystery (#1)

Ava Logan, single mother and small business owner, lives deep in the heart of the Appalachian Mountains, where poverty and pride reign. As publisher of the town newspaper, she's busy balancing election season stories and a rash of ginseng thieves.

And then the story gets personal. After her friend is murdered, Ava digs for the truth all the while juggling her two teenage children, her friend's orphaned toddler, and her own muddied past. Faced with threats against those closest to her, Ava must find the killer before she, or someone she loves, ends up dead.

Available at booksellers nationwide and online

Visit www.henerypress.com for details

FATAL BRUSHSTROKE

Sybil Johnson

An Aurora Anderson Mystery (#1)

A dead body in her garden and a homicide detective on her doorstep...

Computer programmer and tole-painting enthusiast Aurora (Rory) Anderson doesn't envision finding either when she steps outside to investigate the frenzied yipping coming from her own back yard. After all, she lives in Vista Beach, a quiet California beach community where violent crime is rare and murder even rarer.

Suspicion falls on Rory when the body buried in her flowerbed turns out to be someone she knows—her tole-painting teacher, Hester Bouquet. Just two weeks before, Rory attended one of Hester's weekend seminars, an unpleasant experience she vowed never to repeat. As evidence piles up against Rory, she embarks on a quest to identify the killer and clear her name. Can Rory unearth the truth before she encounters her own brush with death?

Available at booksellers nationwide and online

Visit www.henerypress.com for details

CROPPED TO DEATH

Christina Freeburn

A Faith Hunter Scrap This Mystery (#1)

Former US Army JAG specialist, Faith Hunter, returns to her West Virginia home to work in her grandmothers' scrapbooking store determined to lead an unassuming life after her adventure abroad turned disaster. But her quiet life unravels when her friend is charged with murder—and Faith inadvertently supplied the evidence. So Faith decides to cut through the scrap and piece together what really happened.

With a sexy prosecutor, a determined homicide detective, a handful of sticky suspects and a crop contest gone bad, Faith quickly realizes if she's not careful, she'll be the next one cropped.

Available at booksellers nationwide and online

Visit www.henerypress.com for details

CPSIA information can be obtained
at www.ICGtesting.com
Printed in the USA
LVOW10s0240110418
573059LV00022B/872/P